The Adventures of Charlie Pierce

Charlie and the Tycoon

by Harvey E. Oyer III

Illustrations by James Balkovek

Map Illustration by Jeanne Brady

www.TheAdventuresofCharliePierce.com

Become a friend of Charlie Pierce on Facebook

MIDDLE
RIVER
PRESS

ISBN 978-0-9964086-7-7

Copyright © 2016 by Harvey E. Oyer III

Published by:
Middle River Press
Oakland Park, Florida
middleriverpress.com.
info@middleriverpress.com

Printed in the U.S.A.
First printing

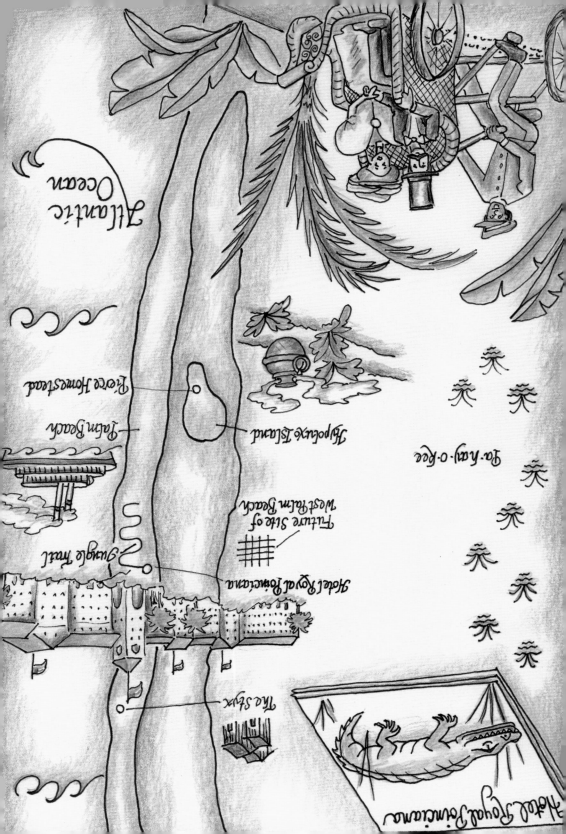

Dedication

To my mother, for all that she sacrificed for me.

Acknowledgments

I wish to acknowledge the dedicated, outstanding work of editor Jon VanZile, illustrator James Balkovek, MFA, map illustrator Jeanne Brady, and the folks at Middle River Press. I also want to acknowledge the writings of Charles W. Pierce and Lillie Pierce Voss, from which I take many of the stories contained herein. My special thanks to John M. Blades, Executive Director Emeritus, Flagler Museum, and Dr. Thomas Graham, Professor of History Emeritus, Flagler College, for their review of the manuscript and helpful comments. Finally, a special thanks to Jason Gonzalez, great-grandson of Alfonso Fernando Gonzalez, for sharing his family's rich history and allowing portions of it to be used in this book.

Introduction

This is the fifth book in a series of books about the adventures of young Charlie Pierce, one of South Florida's earliest pioneer settlers. The story follows teenaged Charlie and his fearless little sister, Lillie, in the late 1800s, when South Florida was America's last frontier. Together with his Seminole friend, Tiger, Charlie experienced one of the most intriguing and exotic lives imaginable. His adventures as a young boy growing up in the wild, untamed jungles of Florida became legendary. Perhaps no other person experienced firsthand as many important events and met as many influential characters in South Florida's history.

For more information about the Pierce family's adventures, go to
www.TheAdventuresofCharliePierce.com
Become a friend of Charlie Pierce on **Facebook**
Facebook.com/CharliePierceBooks

Table of Contents

Chapter One

A Steamboat Surprise

It was still dark outside when I was awakened by a soft scuffling sound in the hallway. I opened my eyes and listened as our front door softly opened and shut. Then I groaned.

Lillie was sneaking out again.

I put my pillow over my head, but it was no use. I'd never get back to sleep, even though it was still before dawn. Annoyed, I threw my covers off and swung my feet out of bed. This time I was going to give Lillie a piece of my mind.

I followed my sister's path through the dark house and out the front door. The half-moon was low on the horizon when I stepped onto our porch. Just as I suspected, Lillie was on the other side of our yard, perched on a log with her sketchbook and pencils on her lap. She was staring intently into the wild and dark jungle, no doubt looking for an animal to sketch. I stomped across the yard toward her.

She looked up at me and frowned. "Quiet!" she whispered.

I looked around, half expecting to see a panther crouched and ready to spring. "What am I being quiet for?" I asked in a loud whisper. "There's nothing out here except you."

"I'm not the one making all the noise!"

"Lillie, this is—"

"*Look!*"

I whirled around and squinted into the trees. The jungle was a dark tangle of trunks and shadows. I thought I saw something big moving silently through the trees. Whatever it was, it didn't make any noise.

"You see it?" Lillie whispered excitedly.

"What is it?"

"I think it's a black bear. I found his prints in the woods."

"A bear? Here?"

"Yeah. I think he comes here every morning, before we wake up, looking for food. I wish I had some berries or something to get him to come out. I just want to see him!"

"Lillie," I said in a warning voice, "you'd better not bring a bear close to the house on purpose. Papa would have a heart attack and then he'd—"

Suddenly, the morning silence was shattered by a high-pitched whistle that echoed over the

"Charlie," Lillie said. "Is that a ... steamboat?"

"I think so," I said. "What's a steamboat doing here?"

Lillie didn't answer, and we waited until we could see the little boat chugging slowly down the lake toward us. It wasn't much larger than Uncle Will's sailboat, with high gunwales and a little cabin. Stubby twin brass smokestacks puffed out white steam every few minutes.

"We should get Papa," Lillie said.

But before we could, the front door banged open and Papa came out pulling up his suspenders, his hair still sticking up and his eyes

13

lake. There was a loud crashing in the trees as the big animal ran away. Lillie jumped to her feet. We both strained our eyes to look up the lake and find out where the whistle came from.

"What was that?" she asked.

"I don't know, but it sure scared your bear away."

We scanned the lake's dark water. Several minutes later, I saw a pinprick of golden light on the horizon, like a ghostly light floating over the water. The sun was coming up faster now, and the morning was turning from black to gray. The ghostly light on the water soon revealed itself to be a lantern swinging from a pole and illuminating the deck of the most unusual ship I had ever seen on our lake.

bleary with sleep. He jumped in surprise when he saw us already outside.

"I heard a whistle just now," he said. "What are you two doing up and out already? And what is that?" He motioned at the steamboat in the distance.

"I don't know," I said. "But it's headed this way."

Papa squinted into the morning light. "Well, I'll be. You just never know what you'll see."

"You know whose it is?" Lillie asked.

Papa shook his head. "No. Can't say that I do. But they sure aren't in a hurry to get here. That's just about the slowest boat I've ever seen."

It took a few more minutes before I heard the first faint chugging of the little boat's engine.

"Okay, children," Papa said. "It'll be a while before they get here. Plenty of time to grab a bite to eat before we see who it is."

Chapter Two

The Tycoon Drops By

Lillie and I went inside and found Mama making biscuits for breakfast. After we ate, Lillie and I crowded around the front window to watch the little boat getting closer and closer. The boat's wheelhouse gleamed with brass fixtures, and the boat was freshly painted white that shined like coral rock in the dawn. The trim was painted a pretty red.

Without asking permission, Lillie pushed through the front door and went outside. I followed her, and we stood next to Papa.

Mama came last, shielding her eyes against the sun to look at the funny little boat. Pretty soon, we could see the name *Adelante* stenciled on the bow and two men standing on the front deck. They were both wearing suit jackets and vests—that by itself was strange enough. I could count on one hand the number of times I'd seen men dressed in suits.

"You think they're from Tallahassee?" I asked Papa.

He shook his head. "Don't know why government men would want to come visit us. Besides, that doesn't look like any government boat."

A third man popped out of the wheelhouse to join the others on deck. He wore coarse work pants but had on a blue mariner's jacket and a little peaked cap. He waved an arm and his voice carried across the water toward us. "Ahoy!" he hailed. "Morning to you!"

We exchanged a glance and headed down the path to our small dock. Papa waved back at the visitors as we neared the dock. "You coming to tie up?" Papa yelled. "Just make sure to come in slow so you don't reduce my dock to kindling!"

"Hold for a minute!" the captain yelled, ducking into the wheelhouse to throttle the engines back. The boat drifted sideways as it slowed down, coming into our dock pushing a big wave of water and trailing steam from the shiny smokestacks.

We'd seen a lot of strange characters tie up to our dock over the years—from Yale professors to wild-eyed plume hunters—but watching this steamboat bear down on our dock was surely one of the strangest sights yet.

The little steamer dwarfed our dock, and I was sure it would crash right into the old wood and send me, Lillie, Mama, and Papa into the water. But at the last minute, the captain threw the engine into reverse. A great puff of

17

smoke rose as the boat came to a near stop. A second later, the captain darted from the cabin and threw me a rope. I caught it and looped it around one of the pilings.

The steamboat docked just as softly as a leaf falling on the ground. I was impressed.

Throughout this whole procedure, the two men on the deck watched us without a word. Up close, they looked like they might have been brothers, one younger and one older. They both had severe parts in their hair and wore moustaches. The younger of the two had curled up the ends of his moustache and was deeply tanned, like he had spent many years in the sun. The older man looked familiar to me, but I couldn't remember where I'd met him before. He wore a stern expression, with deep-set, piercing eyes under thick eyebrows. His moustache was neatly trimmed and close. He looked at each of us in turn, and when I made eye contact with him, he seemed to be studying me. I found I couldn't hold his gaze for long without looking down.

There was a thud as the captain busied himself with a hand crank to lower a short gangplank. "Thank you," he said to me. "If you please, my passengers are looking for the Pierce property. They're wanting to meet Mr. Charlie Pierce, the boy who delivered the mail down here."

"Mr. Charlie?" I said in surprise. "That's me."

his partner, John D. Rockefeller. He'd come to Florida recently. In the last few years, Flagler had built two large hotels in St. Augustine. After that, he bought a few smaller railroads heading south to Daytona and bought another hotel near there.

People said his hotels were more like castles than regular buildings. Cap Dimick said that Flagler's biggest hotel in St. Augustine, the Ponce de Leon, had cost $2.5 million to build. It didn't seem possible to me that one man had that much money.

It seemed even more amazing that Henry Flagler was at that very moment strolling down the gangplank and onto our dock, followed by Mr. James Ingraham. I suspect Papa was

"Nice to make your acquaintance, Mr. Pierce," the captain said to me, and then he turned to Papa. "My name is Franklin White. I'd like to introduce you to my employers, Mr. James Ingraham and Mr. Henry Flagler."

Flagler!

I heard Mama gasp and, from the corner of my eye, saw her hand flutter up to her hair, which she had tied in a loose kerchief.

Papa's eyes widened slightly, and even Lillie looked surprised.

Everybody in our area had heard of Henry Flagler. He had become a millionaire after he created an oil company called Standard Oil with

thinking the same thing as Mr. Flagler extended his hand in introduction.

I was suddenly aware of the shabby work clothes Papa and I wore, compared to their fine suits. Papa even had a long machete strapped to his waist. He'd taken to wearing one after a rattlesnake bit him in our cane field last year.

"Mr. Pierce," Flagler said, his voice deep and commanding. "It's a pleasure to make your acquaintance."

"Thank you," Papa said. "Uh, sorry ... we, uh, weren't expecting company this morning, and I'm afraid—"

Flagler waved the apology aside. "No, no. I should be the one apologizing to you for dropping in unannounced like this. Fact is, we've been water-testing the *Adelante* and thought the very early morning was the best time for a cruise. Water's calmer, they say, and the alligators are sleeping." He spoke slowly and deliberately, like he had carefully considered every word he was going to say.

"Alligators? Sleeping?" Papa stammered, and I looked at him in wonder. I'd never seen Papa at a loss for words.

"Just a joke!" Flagler said. "Except about that boat. You'd be surprised how difficult it was to get that little craft down here and through the inlet into your lake. But it's for the better. I've been fascinated by steam lately. I just finished

building the *Alicia*. She's a two-masted steam yacht with a three-cylinder steam engine, much bigger than this little boat."

"A steam yacht?" Mama echoed, plainly confused.

"Mrs. Pierce I presume," Flagler said, taking off his hat and bowing slightly toward her. "I'm sorry, I seem to be getting ahead of myself. In fact, this visit has a purpose. Myself and Mr. Ingraham here wanted to come by this morning and thank your son."

"Thank Charlie?" Mama said.

Flagler turned to me and I tried not to gulp nervously. I'd never met a millionaire before, and I wasn't sure if I was supposed to know some type

of millionaire greeting. Everything Mama had ever taught me about manners suddenly emptied from my head.

"Yes, ma'am," Flagler said. "We heard that young Charlie here prevented a certain set of maps and documents from falling into the wrong hands not too long ago. I wanted to meet this brave and enterprising boy for myself and give him a proper thank-you."

"Oh, uh . . ." Now I found myself stammering, desperately trying to remember what he was talking about, even though it was only last year that our good friend Hamilton had disappeared while trying to deliver a set of plans to Miami. They outlined Mr. Flagler's plan to buy land for a possible rail track all the way south. Lillie and I had been chased down the coast by two thugs hired by a man named Gleason. In the end, Hamilton had switched the plans and the thugs stole a set of fakes.

I never found out if Mr. Flagler had bought that land or not, but that was how I became a Barefoot Mailman. Thankfully, my mail contract had just ended, so my days of walking miles down the beach every week were over.

"Oh my!" Mama said. "Where are my manners? I'm sure you two would prefer to come in out of the sun. Come inside and have some juice and breakfast, if you please. I've got some biscuits still warm in the oven."

"Thank you," Flagler said. "That sounds wonderful."

So that's how we ended up leading Mr. Henry Flagler up the narrow dirt path from our little dock and into our thatch-roof house. When he reached the porch, he stopped and waited for Mr. Ingraham, who so far hadn't said more than a couple words of greeting. They stood side by side for a minute, surveying the view of our island and lake from the porch. An osprey hovered overhead and the waters of the lake shone in the strengthening sun. Mr. Flagler took a deep breath and broke into a smile.

"I will say, Mr. and Mrs. Pierce, you've managed to set yourselves up on a corner of paradise!" He and Mr. Ingraham exchanged a glance. "Now, let's see about those biscuits."

Chapter Three

Pennies for Progress

"Mrs. Pierce, I have to say this is a delicious jelly. What did you say it was made from again? I've never had a jelly quite like it." Mr. Flagler said this as he slathered more of Mama's clear jelly on his warm biscuit.

"It's sea grape," she said. "I used to wish for berries like we had in Chicago, but I could never get raspberries or blueberries to grow here. It's too hot and humid. But the sea grape trees have an excellent fruit that works just as well."

Flagler took another bite of his biscuit, closed his eyes in appreciation while he chewed, then smiled. "You see," he said, "it's moments like this that only reinforce my opinion of this paradise. I'm convinced, and I believe experience has proven me correct, that there's tremendous interest among our shivering friends up north to come down here and see this Eden for themselves."

"Seems like an awful out-of-the-way place for most people," Papa said.

Flagler nodded. "For now, for now. But I believe that's changing quickly. In fact, my colleague here, Mr. Ingraham, recently spent several weeks in your western swamp, looking for a way to get a railroad from the west side of the state over to this side of the peninsula. The race is on, as they say."

"Bring a railroad across the swamp?" Papa said.

James Ingraham nodded. "Yes, but my trip showed us how impossible that would be. Your swamp isn't a swamp at all, but a shallow and wide river that could no sooner be dredged than the tide could be stopped. Anyone who wanted to build a railroad through there would have to put it on trestles all the way across."

"Not to mention deal with the snakes and gators," Lillie chimed in.

Flagler smiled at her. "Yes, and that's not to mention the snakes and gators."

"But why would you want to build a railroad through the swamp?" I asked.

"Oh, no, it wasn't me," Flagler said. "Are you familiar with Henry Plant up in the northern part of your state?"

We shook our heads.

"Well, Mr. Plant is what you might call a friend and rival of mine. He's been laying railroads and building hotels through the center of Florida, heading toward the west coast. He just opened up the Tampa Bay Hotel near the Gulf of Mexico. From what I hear, the hotel has been an unqualified success. Naturally, his ambition is to arrive here before me."

"Arrive here?" Papa said. "But … you're here right now."

Flagler laughed. "Oh, no, I don't mean in person. I mean … Well, perhaps I can show you. Considering as you're residents here, I'd be happy to count you among my friends and supporters."

This seemed like a strange request, but it only took one look around the table to see that we were all curious.

"Well, alright," Papa said. "What is it you have to show us?"

"Come," Flagler said, eating the last of his biscuit and flicking crumbs away from his moustache. "Let's go for a boat ride."

Before long, we were chugging up the lake on the *Adelante*. I'd never been on any type of steamboat before and found the thrum of the engines soothing. Lillie sat near the stern with her sketchpad, drawing the wheelhouse. Mama and Papa were installed in deck chairs next to her. I found myself up near the bow, leaning on the railing and watching the clear water slide under the boat. The shore was a wild profusion of plants growing so thickly they sometimes formed a shelf of vegetation over the water.

"You mind if I join you?"

I looked around and was surprised to see Mr. Flagler rounding the corner of the wheelhouse.

"No, sir," I said.

He leaned against the railing and stared at the lakeshore for a few minutes before he said, "You know, I've heard some good things about you. Sounds like you're an enterprising young man."

"Enterprising?"

"When I heard that a boy and his little sister left their home to head out alone and help a friend, I sent out inquiries," Flagler said. "From what I heard, you're my kind of boy.

I left my own home when I was fourteen years old. I said good-bye to my parents and sailed from New York, where I was born, to Sandusky, Ohio, to work in my cousin's general store. I took everything I owned in a bag with me, and it wasn't a large bag." He laughed to himself.

"Turned out I wasn't much of a sailor either. I was so sick on the way down that lake, I thought I might toss up my own lungs. Of course, it was a much bigger lake than this one, so big it was like an ocean. When I finally did arrive at my cousin's store to start working, I counted all the money I had in the world. It was a grand total of nine cents and one coin from France that might as well have been a rock for all the value it had in Ohio. That's a feeling I never forgot, what it's like to have only nine cents to my name. I vowed I'd never feel that way again. Since then, I would say

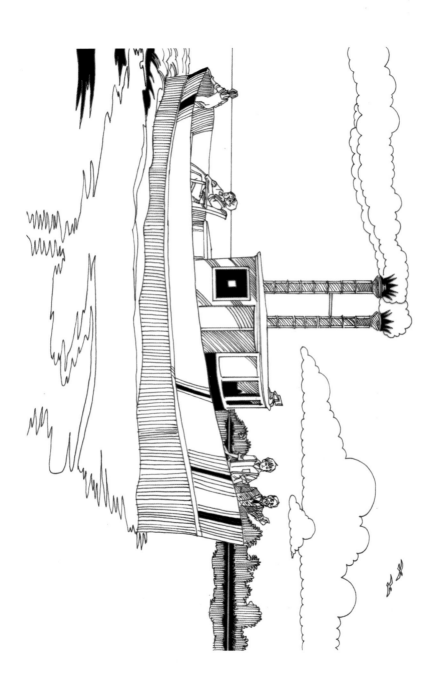

I've been contented with my life, but I've never been satisfied."

"We don't have much money," I offered, not sure what he was trying to tell me.

Flagler looked at me from under his deep eyebrows. "But you have something else that I think many other people would value. Have you ever been up to St. Augustine?"

"No, sir. We can't be away from the farm that long."

He nodded. "I can appreciate that. But if you did see it, you'd see what I mean. It's a beautiful city now. A bustling city. The hotel we built up there, the Ponce de Leon, has been bursting with people since it opened." He paused. "You remember what I said about Mr. Plant in Tampa and myself in a little bit of a race?"

"Yes, sir."

"Well, here's what I mean. You see there?" He pointed to a stretch of shore that looked much like the rest: tangled trees and vines, crystal clear water lapping at the shore. "I want you to imagine a building there, but not just any building. The grandest hotel the world has ever seen. Five hundred rooms. Gardens that would rival anything in ancient Babylon. People strolling along the lakeshore on wooden walkways, and lanterns glowing on jungle trails. And of course, boats touring the lake."

I laughed despite myself. "It sounds nice, Mr. Flagler. But I don't think it's possible to build anything like that here. Just clearing the land would take months. Then it would take a hundred shipwrecks to get that much wood."

Mr. Flagler laughed. "I've heard that shipwrecks are an important part of the economy here! But, Charlie, I'm not the type who trusts my fortunes to storms and other men's misfortune. Right now as we speak, I've got teams of men clearing a path for a railroad that will run straight down from Daytona to that very spot. At the same time, the first building supplies are being loaded onto steamers bound from Eau Gallie to Jupiter, then onto your little railroad from Jupiter to Juno. When they start arriving, we'll have enough supplies to break ground on the world's biggest, most beautiful hotel.

"I put my teams to a challenge, to see if the railway men can reach this place before the hotel is finished. Now, if you think about all those men heading down this way, and you put your imagination to it, I suspect you'll see just what I'm talking about."

I stared again at the wild and familiar lakeshore and let his words sink in. And then, suddenly, it was like a light had turned on in a dark room and I saw it exactly as he'd described it: the grand hotel like a castle, the people in their evening clothes walking under swinging lanterns, small boats merrily scooting over the lake. It was like he had put a picture straight into my head, and my heart beat faster with a mixture of apprehension and excitement.

Flagler smiled. "I recognize that look," he said. "It's the look that fuels progress."

I looked at the man next to me—one of the richest, most powerful people in the whole country—and was surprised to realize that I felt comfortable with him, even friendly. And maybe that's what led me to say the first thing that popped into my mind: "Papa's not very keen on progress. Says it's too crowded."

Now Mr. Flagler really laughed. "Young man, if I had a penny for every man who felt that way, I could buy up the whole of Florida!"

Chapter Four

A Scene from Dante's Inferno

After Mr. Flagler and Mr. Ingraham dropped us off at home, Papa's thoughts turned immediately back to me and Lillie. He wanted to know exactly why both of his kids had been outside before dawn. Lillie was forced to confess that she'd been getting up every day to sketch wild animals and she was convinced there was a bear on our island.

Papa was naturally alarmed. Black bears were known to roam the woods throughout Florida. Many families had stories of bears

breaking into their houses or storehouses and stealing their food. The last thing any of us wanted was for Mama to wake up in the morning and find a hungry bear in her kitchen.

It took only a few minutes' searching in the woods to find bear droppings scattered along the trail that led up the island. Papa stood over a big pile of scat, looking concerned.

"Alright, Charlie and Lillie," he said. "At

the first opportunity, we're going out to track this bear. See if we can find where it's living."

And that's how we ended up—me, Lillie, and Papa—trekking softly through the woods just after dawn a week later, heading to the north end of the island.

Lillie was ahead of us, her head bent to the ground so she could track the bear, while Papa and I followed. I had my favorite rifle, Ol' Lauderdale, in my hands, while Papa had an old shotgun slung over his shoulder.

"Now, you remember, Charlie, if we see that bear, we're not to shoot it," Papa warned me for the tenth time. "A wounded bear is far more dangerous than a whole one."

I nodded in agreement. With only Doc Potter for medical care, a bear attack could be deadly.

We followed the path all the way to the northeast side of Hypoluxo Island, where a narrow strip of lake separated our island from the barrier island. We gathered on the shore where the path ended and looked across to the windswept dunes and thick clusters of sea oats and sea grapes on the other side.

"You think he's over there?" I asked.

Papa shrugged. "Perhaps. But we're still pretty early in turtle season. Without a good supply of turtle eggs to keep him busy, he'll lose interest and come back here."

"What do we do?"

"Don't know just yet," Papa said. "Keep an eye out, I suppose. Either he's over there or he's still back in the woods behind us. Truth is, if that bear doesn't want to get seen in broad daylight, we'll never find him."

"Papa?" Lillie cut in. "Is that smoke?"

We turned to look where Lillie was pointing, due north. Sure enough, black smoke was climbing up the horizon, flattening out as it went up and blowing in tatters toward Pa-Hay-Okee.

Papa frowned. "Oh boy," he said grimly. "Seems like one surprise after another this week, and none of them welcome."

Lillie and I exchanged a worried glance. It was still the dry season, and fire was always a problem in South Florida. It rained half the year, but we were dry as the Sahara for the other half of the year. Great fires often burned on the horizon and stained the night sky red. If the wind shifted and the fires came too close to the shore, Papa would make us haul bucket after bucket of water from the lake and douse our roof until it was soggy. The last thing we wanted was a stray ember caught on the breeze to float down and set our house afire.

"You think we should go take a look?" I ventured.

Papa thought it over, then agreed. "I hate the prospect of losing a whole day's work, but yes,

34

I guess we better check on our neighbors up that way, make sure everyone is safe and sound."

***

It took the better part of the morning to work our way back home, then sail up the lake in our little boat. The smoke continued to build on the horizon. Whatever was burning up there, it was getting bigger.

As we neared the source of the fire, Lillie and I left Papa at the tiller and crowded up front. I had expected to find a field of dry pine on fire, but instead we saw that a gash had been cut into the thick growth of the eastern lakeshore and a large area of newly cleared land extended back into the jungle. Newly cut trees littered the ground, and dozens of men darted through the heavy smoke, carrying saws, chains, and ropes. They

were digging up stumps, lopping branches off the downed trees, and dragging the wood to the back of the clearing. There we saw the source of the black smoke: they had built the biggest bonfire I'd ever seen, the flames licking forty feet into the air.

"My goodness," Papa said quietly. "It's like a scene straight from Dante's Inferno. I can almost feel the heat from here."

I knew what he meant. Despite the light sea breeze, I could feel the heat pulling at my skin.

"Papa?" Lillie said. "Who are those men?"

That's when I first looked closely at the men themselves. To protect themselves from floating cinders and sharp branches, most of them were wrapped head to toe in long pants and shirts, only leaving bits of their skin exposed. It took me a second to realize that almost all of the men in the jungle clearing were black.

It was an unusual thing to see great numbers of black people in our area. There were only a few black settlers. There was Mama's friend Aunt Betsy, the midwife who had delivered Lillie as a baby. Then there were Fannie and Samuel James, who lived in a new settlement on the lake called Jewell, where Fannie was the postmistress. And Millie Gildersleeve was another midwife who delivered babies with Doc Potter for families around the lake. She had been a slave in Georgia before she won her freedom and moved here.

Then there were the Black Seminoles, who

were mostly escaped slaves who joined the Seminole tribe. They had lived in the jungle and swamps for many years, but they stuck to themselves and almost never had contact with the rest of the settlers.

But the men in the field were all strangers, and I wondered where they had come from. At least some of them had to be freed slaves. I looked at Papa.

The War Between the States had deeply affected my family. Before they moved south, both Papa and Uncle Will had fought for the Union. They both were in the Union Army with the Seventh Illinois Cavalry from 1863 to 1865. They had fought in Tennessee and believed in the abolitionist cause to end slavery.

Papa sent us skimming over the water toward the shore. The smell of smoke hung heavy in the air, and the crash and clatter of men working echoed across the water.

Mr. Ingraham looked up and saw us coming. His tanned face split into a grin, and he waded into knee-deep water to throw us a rope. I caught it while he waded back and tied us to a tree by the water. Once we were tied up, we jumped into the clear water and waded ashore to join Mr. Ingraham and the men at the table. Mr. Ingraham introduced us around, and a tough-looking man with a big, swept-back moustache rose up to shake Papa's hand.

"Joseph McDonald, foreman," he said.

Papa, however, hardly seemed to notice the working men. Instead, he was staring hard at the shore. Then he said, "Isn't that Mr. Ingraham?"

I followed his gaze and saw where a rough table had been set up under the trees at the edge of the clearing. A large barrel was positioned next to the table. Mr. Ingraham sat at the table surrounded by a group of men in sweat-stained shirts and suspenders. These men were all white. They had rolls of paper spread out on the table, held down at the corners with stones, and pored over them like treasure hunters. Mr. Ingraham seemed to be giving directions. As I watched, a few of them got up and headed back into the clearing to give instructions to workers.

"This is the man who built the Ponce de Leon," Ingraham explained. "He's in charge here."

As we settled around the table, a steady stream of men from the field wandered over to the barrel for a drink. A broad wood ladle hung on the edge, so the men could dip out a cupful of water at a time and satisfy their thirst or wash the dirt and ashes from their faces. I noticed that Mr. McDonald nodded at every man who came over, and they returned the courtesy with smiles.

"That's hot and sweaty work," Papa observed, looking into the field where a group of six men were leaning their weight into a chain to tear a big tree stump out of the ground.

"I reckon so," McDonald said. "But they're hoping to make that fire even higher. A few of the men plan to head out later and see if they can find a wild boar and have themselves a roast. What do you think? They'll have any luck?"

"Maybe," Papa allowed, watching the cutting and burning. "There are plenty of hogs in these woods, but with all this racket, it's hard to imagine the pig who'll stick around. Any animal for that matter." He paused. "Your Mr. Flagler sure is in a hurry. Just a few days ago this land was pristine."

McDonald gave a smile. "Yes, indeed," he said. "When Mr. Flagler puts his mind to something, it's bound to happen in record time. Today is May first, and the plan is to have the hotel fully operational by this winter."

"That's mighty fast," Papa said.

"Indeed. In fact, it's a fortunate turn of events you showed up today," Ingraham picked up. "We've got a list a mile long of things that need doing, and we're going to need plenty of help. Charlie, Mr. Flagler instructed me to drop by your house with a job offer."

"A job offer?" I echoed as Papa and Lillie looked surprised. "What kind of job?" I sincerely hoped it didn't involve walking up and down the beach again.

"Oh, I suspect it's a job you'll like. What do you say? Are you open to becoming a Flagler man?"

I nodded before I could think twice about it, but not before I saw a crease wrinkle Papa's forehead.

Chapter Five

Uncorking the Tornado

It turned out Mr. Ingraham was right: my new job was exactly the kind of job I liked.

Instead of walking to Miami every week, I would get to work at the hotel site, where Mr. Ingraham said they were building an exotic Jungle Trail for the hotel guests. My job was to mark out the path where the Jungle Trail would go, sticking to the areas that wouldn't flood during the coming rainy season and wash away the path.

When the Jungle Trail was done, Mr. Ingraham said hotel guests could pay to ride a special type of wheeled cart through the heavy jungle. The carts would be pedaled by hotel employees, with two riders per cart.

I'd never heard of any such thing before, but if it was a Jungle Trail they wanted, it would be a Jungle Trail they got. So every morning, I'd get up around dawn, complete my chores on the farm, then sail north on my boat, *Oriole*, and spend the afternoon trekking

41

through the dense growth south of the future hotel. I did my best to guess where the water would flow when it rained, then I marked the trees with red paint where I thought the path should go.

When I told Papa what they'd hired me to do, he just raised his eyebrows and shook his head.

"No matter how many ways I try to think about it, I just can't figure a path to nowhere where men push around other people in fancy carts like dray horses," he remarked. "It's not dignified for either party, the pusher or the pushed. And this isn't even to mention the fact that I don't see anyone lining up around here to get pushed through a jungle infested with insects, snakes, gators, and all manner of living things."

The way I saw it, the forest wouldn't be infested with all manner of living things by the time Flagler's men were done. They were clearing and burning at record pace. They were busy in two spots: the first was a clearing just north of the hotel, where they were building shacks for themselves to live in. They were calling this area The Styx, just like in Greek mythology.

The second spot was where they'd build the hotel. The more time I spent around the work site, the deeper my amazement grew. Even though he had gone back north, Mr. Flagler seemed to hang over every sentence and scene.

Everywhere I went, I could hear men saying "Mr. Flagler wants this ... " or "Mr. Flagler wants that ..."

To hear the men talk about it, Mr. Flagler had personally planned every nail, every board, and every inch of the building rising from the sandy ground like a great wooden honeycomb. I was amazed by the incredible energy and industry of the men—and the number of them. More workers arrived every day, both white and black. I could scarcely understand how one man, even a very rich man like Mr. Flagler, had the energy and vision to unleash all this activity with just a word. I grew to think of him like a genie who had uncorked a tornado.

At home, I didn't talk much about Mr. Flagler, the hotel, or the men streaming in by the dozens. I could tell that Papa wasn't excited about it, and it didn't help much when Lillie started complaining about the smoke on the horizon or the men cutting down her forest.

Things got a little better when word got around that Mr. Flagler was sponsoring a drawing contest for a poster promoting the hotel. The prize was fifty dollars, and Lillie immediately decided she was going to not only enter but also win. All she needed was the perfect drawing of a native plant or animal. She announced that was "going to be near impossible with these men scaring all the animals away or killing them," but she went out every day with her sketchpad anyway.

She didn't find her mystery bear, but she did come in one afternoon and report that a dead tarpon almost four feet long had washed up on our shore. It had a hook in its mouth trailing a bit of line and a hole in its side like someone had tried to harpoon it. Papa grunted that only a fool would go after a tarpon with such flimsy line, and there was no reason to kill them anyway. "That's a game fish," he said, "not an eatin' fish. What's the point in killing them?"

Lillie was soon sketching the giant fish and wondering if a tarpon was interesting enough to win Flagler's drawing contest.

"Not a dead one with a hole in its side," I said. "You should draw an alligator. I bet most of those northerners have never seen one."

"Ick," Lillie said. "There's nothing special about alligators. I want something better than a boring old alligator."

I didn't say much. If Lillie was having trouble with her drawing, I wasn't having much more luck with the Jungle Trail. No matter how hard I tried, I couldn't remember where the water flowed during the rainy season. It seemed like every time I laid a path, I remembered another trickle of water from a previous year. I spent one whole day marking trees near the water, only to realize I was below the high summer tide.

Finally, I got lucky. One morning as I pulled the *Oriole* ashore for another afternoon of trekking and marking trees, I saw a familiar figure waiting for me: my Seminole friend Tiger Bowlegs. Tiger's dark hair was pulled into a pony tail that hung down his back, and he wore a colorful shirt with alligator skin patches on the shoulders. His rifle was propped against a tree next to him. He greeted me with a cheerful, "Istonko!"

"Tiger!" I said, grinning. "What are you doing here?"

He nodded toward the nearby clearing, where teams of men were hammering at the wooden skeleton of the hotel. "Wanted to see for myself," he said. "Heard they build hotel here."

"Yeah," I said. "It's Mr. Henry Flagler's new hotel."

Tiger made a grunt. "Big building."

"They say it's going to have more than five hundred guest rooms when it's done."

Tiger shrugged. "No people here. Who will stay in hotel? Herons?" He smiled at his own joke.

"No. Mr. Flagler is building a railroad down here from up north. The hotel team is competing with the railroad team, to see who can finish first. Whoever wins get a cash bonus." I paused. "Hey, can you help me with something? You know how to read the land."

He looked pleased. "What you need help with?"

I explained to him about the Jungle Trail and my trouble with it. When I was done, he agreed to help, even though he declared it was a silly idea. I led him into the woods to show him where I'd been marking trees with red paint.

"This no good," he said. "See this here?" He pointed to a patch of brown leaves piled up on a dead log. "Those special ferns. Only grow when rain comes and water rises. They waiting for rains to come and flood so they

can grow. This place too wet. Have to go further east."

I groaned, but agreed. Tiger and I picked up the can of red paint and headed further east, working our way toward the dune and then looping back south again. As we got further away from the clearing, the sound of hammers, saws, and men working was replaced with the sound of wind in the branches and birdcalls. It was nice walking through the woods with Tiger—I had missed my friend.

After a few hours of marking trees, we were both tired and scratched up from sharp branches. "Time for a break," I announced, and Tiger nodded gratefully.

We decided to cross the dune and go to the beach. We scrambled up the sandy dune, pushing through sea grape and sea oats until we found ourselves standing on the top of the dune, looking down on the sea beyond.

We had expected to find the beach and sea empty, but I was surprised to see a large ocean steamer steering close to shore. It looked like one of the Mallory & Company steamers that passed every few months on the way to Key West. But they had never come this close to shore before.

A man was standing against the steamer's rail scanning the beach with a pair of binoculars. He saw us emerge from the jungle and immediately began waving vigorously

to get our attention. Tiger and I exchanged a confused glance as the air was split with a shrieking whistle and a huge anchor splashed into the sea from the steamer's bow.

"You know that boat?" Tiger said.

I shook my head.

While we watched, a small wooden skiff crashed to the water and sailors tied it up to the side of the steamer. A door opened on the side of the steamer and the small figures of men began to leap from the big steamer into the wooden skiff bobbing alongside.

At the same time, a white flag began to climb the flagpole. I realized what it meant

48

and chills spread up my arms. The flag was white with a small red square in the middle encased on all sides with a blue border.

"Uh oh," I said.

"What?"

"That means they have a medical emergency," I answered. "This can't be good."

Chapter Six

Trouble Steams In

The little skiff had four oars, each manned by a sailor pulling hard and sending the little boat skimming across the surf. A man wearing a smart blue jacket with gold braid stood in the center of the sailors, his arms crossed over his chest.

I was impressed: Even as the little boat rode the waves like a playful dolphin, he never stumbled or sat down. When the boat finally arrived in shallow water, he leaped over the side into knee-deep water with no mind to his black leather boots and waded toward us. I

was surprised to see how young this lieutenant was. He had strawberry blond hair, sideburns growing over his cheeks, and his skin was burned red by the salt spray and sun.

"Ahoy!" he hailed us. "I'm mighty glad to see you boys. We're not familiar with this piece of coast and need some help."

"Help?" I said, looking over his shoulder to the large steamer quietly puffing smoke in deep green water. "How so?"

"We've got some sick men aboard. I heard there are Houses of Refuge around here. Or," he said, looking at Tiger, "maybe you can take us to the nearest medicine man, huh?"

Tiger ignored him.

"We have Houses of Refuge, but they don't have medical supplies or doctors," I said. "What sick men? What kind of sick are they?"

A furtive look crossed the young lieutenant's face. "Well, you know how it is," he said. "Not sure what kind of sick until we see a doctor. But we need to get these men off the boat."

"Men?" I asked. "How many are there?"

"Five or six."

"Um, why don't you wait here and we'll go get some help," I said.

The man's eyes narrowed and he didn't respond for several long heartbeats. Finally, he said, "I reckon that'll be good. In the meantime, we'll start ferrying the sick men to shore."

I nodded quickly, and Tiger and I turned around and jogged back to the dune. Behind us, the young lieutenant climbed back into his boat and they pushed off the beach and started heading back through the surf.

"What's wrong?" Tiger asked as we crested the dune and began to slide down into the jungle on the other side. "You look like you saw ghost."

"I don't know much about sickness," I said, "but Papa told me the yellow fever was up in Jacksonville a few years ago. He said it killed hundreds of people. If those men have yellow fever ..."

I let it trail off. Everybody lived in fear of yellow fever. We had no idea how it spread, but Mama said it was easy to recognize once someone got sick. It started off like a normal sickness, with a fever and aches all over your body. Then you got better after a few days ... except that was a trick the disease played on its victims. Pretty soon it came back—and this second time it was much worse. When the fever came back, people would leak blood and their skin would turn yellow.

Many of them would die.

Tiger made a warding gesture and picked up his pace as we ran back through the jungle to the half-built hotel.

I headed straight for the wooden shack where I knew the foreman, Mr. McDonald spent most of his time. The solid little shack had three steps leading up to a front door, glass windows, and a chimney pipe sticking up from the shingled roof.

Tiger followed me, looking around with wide eyes. All around, men were sawing and cutting and hammering at the huge wooden skeleton that was rising from the ground like a mantis hatching.

Nearby, a great forge had been set up under a makeshift hut. A man wearing a leather apron worked in front of the forge's burning mouth, pounding on a metal tool with a tremendous hammer that clanged against the anvil and sent showers of sparks streaming around his arms.

"What is this place?" Tiger said in an awed voice, but I shushed him and knocked on the shack door. It was opened by a man I didn't recognize. He wore a brown shirt with his shirtsleeves rolled up and suspenders.

"Yes?" he said.

"Is Mr. McDonald here?"

The man called over his shoulder, and soon Mr. McDonald appeared in the doorway, dressed very much like the other man. His big moustache twitched as he looked down at me while I quickly explained about the small boat and the sick men. When I was done, he gathered four or five men and told us to lead him back over the dune to the shore. "And hurry, Charlie," he said. "Last thing we want is yellow fever in camp."

So Tiger and I led the small party through the thick jungle and up the face of the dune. As the ocean came into sight, we saw that two little rowboats were hurrying toward the shore. The young lieutenant was in one boat, while the other had what appeared to be five men huddled under blankets in the center of the boat. The sailors rowing this second boat had covered their faces with rags and seemed like they were in a hurry to get rid of their dangerous cargo of sick men.

When Mr. McDonald saw the two rowboats, he ran down the dune and across the beach, his men following him. They waded right into the water up to their knees and waved their arms, yelling. The sailors in the rowboats seemed to double their efforts to get to shore, angling away from Mr. McDonald to find an open spot of beach.

Then I was shocked to see Mr. McDonald produce a small revolver from his waist and fire a single shot into the air. That got their attention, and the sailors shipped their oars and left their boats bobbing on the waves. The sick men huddled together and looked dismally at us. Even from this far away, standing on the sand, I could see that

their faces were a sickly yellow and they looked thin and diseased.

"You turn back!" Mr. McDonald shouted. "Don't bring those men ashore here!"

The young lieutenant waved his arms and yelled back. "These are sick men!"

"We have no doctors!" Mr. McDonald yelled. "We can't help!"

The lieutenant thought for a second, then said, "Then we'll just leave them ashore and come back later!"

"No, sir, you will not! Those boats will not land on this beach!"

My heart was beating hard as the two parties faced off. I wasn't sure what I thought about this. It seemed cruel to turn away sick men. But I'd heard about yellow fever and the terrible damage it could cause. If those men brought yellow fever into our jungle, it could kill everyone on the lake.

"I can't have them infecting my ship!" the lieutenant finally yelled in frustration, his face going red under his whiskers.

Mr. McDonald didn't respond, but his men fanned out and waded a little bit deeper. The message was clear: they would stop the boats coming ashore by force if they had to.

The lieutenant yelled a few things that would have made Mama blush, then consulted with the sailors on his boat. Meanwhile, the sick men continued to stare at us miserably. I felt bad for them.

Finally, the rowboats turned around and headed back for the steamer without another signal or word.

Mr. McDonald and his men waded back ashore, but they waited by the water until they saw the two rowboats pull alongside the steamer and all the men climb aboard. The great steamer soon belched a black cloud of coal smoke, then white steam hissed out from its stacks and the anchor rose from the depths. Moments later, the steamer began to glide away, a row of sailors watching from the top deck and the water churning in its wake.

"Well, a little, I guess. Those men … they looked pretty sick."

McDonald nodded gravely. "I suppose they are," he said. "But there was nothing we could do to help them. At least until we get decent rail service down here, we might as well be in the deepest Amazon. If yellow fever got into my camp, it would rip through my men like a hurricane. God forbid if it got into your family. Telling me was the right thing to do, and turning them away was equally right, as hard as it might have been. Fact is, you might have just saved this project and everyone's life in the process."

When they were gone, Mr. McDonald and his men started to head back. I fell in alongside them.

I was still feeling a confusion of emotions. Mama had always taught us that the moral thing to do was to help people in need, and those sick men needed help. Then again, I knew there was little we could do for them in our primitive jungle, and it was true that yellow fever was a danger to us all. There were no hospitals here, nothing but Seminole medicine and whatever Doc Potter had on hand.

I noticed Mr. McDonald watching me. "You upset, Charlie?"

57

Chapter Seven

No Expenses Spared

The image of the sick men huddled in the boat bothered me all afternoon. Had we really done the right thing turning away men who needed help? That evening, over dinner, I told Mama and Papa what had happened, half expecting Mama to get angry at Mr. McDonald for refusing to help. Instead, she shot Papa a worried glance.

"Oh, goodness," she said. "Can yellow fever travel over water, Papa?"

"I don't reckon," he said slowly. "But no one really knows. Mr. McDonald was right to keep those men offshore. Yellow fever could mean the end of us all."

Lillie had been silent up until now, but her mouth was drawn into a thin line. "Couldn't Doc Potter help them?" she said in a tight voice.

"No, Lillie, dear," Mama said. "Fact is, we don't know what causes yellow fever and we sure don't know how to cure it."

58

Lillie frowned into her plate and bit her lip. After dinner, she went to her stack of drawings without a word. Mama followed her to the little table where she drew by the light of a candle and looked down at the stack of Lillie's art.

"These are fine drawings," Mama said. "Are these all for Mr. Flagler's contest?"

Lillie shrugged. "Yes, I guess so. I like this one best." She shuffled the stack of papers, and I saw they were mostly birds and plants. She held up a drawing of a snowy egret, just like the ones we had seen in Pa-Hay-Okee during our plume-hunting trip.

"What about that one?" I asked, pointing to a drawing on the bottom of the stack.

Lillie set the egret picture down and picked up the one I had pointed to. It showed an alligator curled up on the shore, its mouth hanging open to reveal rows of sharp teeth. "I don't know," she said. "It's just an alligator. I only drew it because you said I should. It's boring. I don't even think I'm going to enter it."

"I like it," Papa said, moving over to look down at her drawings. "You should enter it just in case. Alongside the others, of course," he added hastily.

"I guess I will," she said. Then she turned to me. "Charlie, are you going up there tomorrow morning?"

I nodded. I'd been working on the Jungle Trail for weeks now, and the hotel construction was moving even faster. They were already starting to clear trees from the Jungle Trail, and soon I figured they'd lay the trail itself. I wondered exactly what kind of pedaled vehicles they were planning.

"Good," Lillie said. "Then I'll hitch a ride with you up the lake and give these to Mr. Ingraham myself."

***

It was early afternoon when Lillie and I pushed off in the *Oriole* and sailed up the lake to the hotel. It was a peaceful day with a light breeze, perfect weather for sailing. When we neared the hotel, Lillie gave a low whistle as the giant wooden skeleton came into view. "My

goodness," she said in an awed voice. "Charlie, look at that! It's taller than the tallest tree!"

The original clearing had been expanded to include a huge stretch of the shore. Still, as big as it was, the giant clearing was barely large enough to contain the hotel's wooden skeleton, which easily towered over the raw jungle pressing up against its sides. The structure itself was six stories tall. Workers had already started to build parts of the peaked roof and a large tower in the middle, over a grand entrance that would look over the lake.

Like every other day, workers swarmed over the wooden struts, hammering and sawing and hauling materials to the upper floors with ropes and winches. Materials were stacked everywhere:

too many barrels of nails to count, lumber piled higher than a grown man could reach, great heaps of bricks, stacks of shingles, and barrel after barrel with labels identifying them as paint, lime, tar, and plaster.

More men were driving huge pilings into the water to build a pier that would jut out in front of the hotel. I steered our boat for the bank, aiming for the spot where I usually tied up south of the hotel. As the boat slid onto wet sand, Lillie turned back to me. "Charlie, do you really think they will fill this hotel with people?"

I laughed. "That's the intention."

"I can't imagine it," she said. "What will all those people do?"

"I don't know," I said truthfully. "I guess they'll spend time on the Jungle Trail."

Just then, an unfamiliar voice called my name. I turned to see a young black man working his way down the shore toward our boat. He waved as he came.

"Mr. Charlie?" he called.

"Yes," I said. "That's me."

"Good to hear!" he said. "I been waitin' all mornin' for you to show. Mr. McDonald said I was to meet you here and introduce myself. I'm Haley Mickens."

"Hi, Haley," I said.

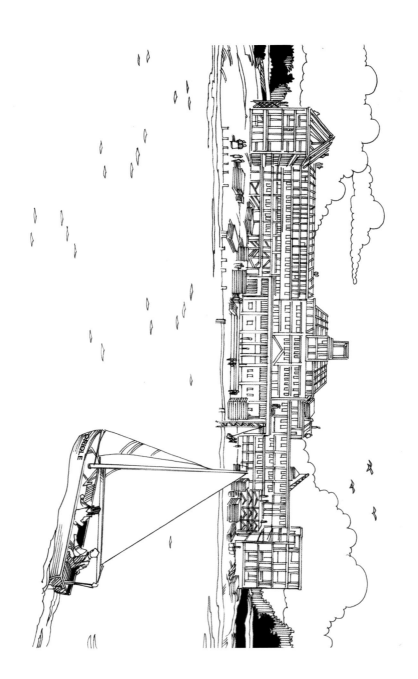

He reached the boat and leaned a hand on the bow while he mopped away sweat from his face with his shirtsleeve. He was dressed in thick work pants supported by suspenders, boots, and a sweat-stained work shirt. On his head he wore a hat he'd woven from palm fronds like the Caribbean islanders did.

"Whew," he said. "It's sure hot today!" He gave a good-natured laugh. "So you're wonderin' why I'm here, no doubt. I was hoping you'd show me the trail and get me a sense of how much pedaling it's going to take. Mr. McDonald says I'm to run the carts on the Jungle Trail when we get this hotel up and running. Yes sir, it turns out you're building my Jungle Trail!"

Mickens looked so happy and proud that I found myself smiling with him. "Sure," I said. "I'll be happy to show you the trail, but I brought my sister, Lillie, up today to deliver her drawings to Mr. Ingraham. Is he here today?"

Mickens grinned at Lillie. "Where are my manners? Hello, Miss Lillie. Why, you're in luck today. It's not just Mr. Ingraham here. Mr. Flagler himself decided to drop in on us today and see how the hotel was coming. I'll walk you up to their building, then you can come back and show me the trail."

We tied the boat up and followed Mickens back up the shoreline, toward the construction shack. Lillie and I waited as Mickens knocked. A face peered briefly through the window, and then Mr. Ingraham opened the door, looking down at me from over his bushy moustache.

"Charlie," he said. "What can we do for you?"

Lillie held up her roll of drawings, which she'd tied with a piece of Mama's ribbon. "I want to enter my drawings in your contest," she said.

Before Ingraham could answer, a voice sounded from the dim cabin beyond. "Enter your drawings? Why don't you bring them in and let us take a look at them right now?"

My heart started beating faintly as I recognized Mr. Flagler's voice. Mr. Ingraham stepped aside and let us walk into the building,

our footsteps echoing on the hollow wood floor. Inside, they had built a large table that was littered with all manner of large plans, pencil nubs, and cups half full of coffee. Two small windows let in a little sunlight. In one corner they had placed a potbellied iron stove that sat cold and empty.

Mr. Flagler was at the table, with architectural drawings spread out before him, including a large drawing of the finished hotel. The drawing showed all six stories painted a pale yellow, with shutters flung open on row after row of windows. A graceful avenue of trees led to the front door, which was flanked by columns that rose two stories into the air to support a covered entry. At the top of it all, an American flag fluttered from the high tower.

"What do you think?" Mr. Flagler said, watching as Lillie and I stared openmouthed at the building. "When it opens, I expect it will be one of the finest hotels in the country."

"It's wonderful," I said. I pointed at the tower on top of the drawing. "Will people be able to climb up there? I sure would love to see what it looks like from so high up!"

Flagler chuckled. "Well, yes, I suppose they will be able to climb up there," he said. "At least the staff."

"Oh," I said, disappointed.

"I imagine you're right, though," he said in his deliberate, slow voice. "It would be something to see this jungle from a hundred feet up." He paused. "I tell you, it does me a wonder of good to see the enthusiasm of youth. Reporters have been asking me for years why a man my age would get into the business of building hotels. My answer is always the same. For many years, I devoted myself exclusively to business. Now I'm pleasing myself, cost what that may."

"How much does it cost?" Lillie asked suddenly. "Mama said your hotel in St. Augustine cost two and a half million dollars."

"Lillie!" I said, horrified that she had asked such a blunt question. "I'm sorry, Mr. Flagler—"

"No, no," he said. "It's fine. I respect a strong-headed young woman. Truth is, we don't have the exact expense yet, but rest assured that we're leaving nothing to chance. Electric lighting. Every detail perfect. Miss Lillie, we'll turn this paradise of yours into the envy of the world."

I'd never met anyone quite like Mr. Flagler before. He seemed to have the ability to turn simple words into a living reality, to transform a flat drawing into a real building. I could almost hear the sound of music drifting from the open front doors and see the graceful ladies in their long dresses and men in suits walking along the entrance path.

"So," Mr. Flagler said, breaking into my thoughts, "you said something about drawings for our little contest? Let us see what you've got."

Lillie untied the ribbon and unrolled the stack of drawings. Flagler and Mr. Ingraham took their time going through the stack, gazing at the different plants, animals, and birds. When they got to the alligator drawing, Flagler whistled. "Now, that's an alligator!"

"Looks like it could eat a full-grown cow," Mr. Ingraham said.

Lillie's face was clouded with disappointment. I knew she hadn't even wanted to bring the alligator, and it was the only one they commented on. Fortunately, she held her tongue.

As they went to gather up the drawings, Mr. Ingraham glanced at me. "I see you met Haley

"Mickens," he began. "He told you he's going to be running the pedaled cart concession for the Jungle Trail?"

"Yes, sir."

"Good. In the meantime, we were hoping you'd do something new for us."

"What is it?"

"You've no doubt seen the work camp the men are calling The Styx. It's good for now, but we'll need a more permanent town for the people who will work in the hotel. We'd like you to run these plans for a new town up to the county seat at the Juno Courthouse."

"A new town?" I asked. "Where?"

"On the west lakeshore," Ingraham said. "We're planning to called it Westpalmbeach and had George Potter draw up a plat that we need to record with the county government. What do you say? You up for a little trip to the north end of the lake?"

"Sure," I said.

Mr. Ingraham handed Lillie her stack of drawings and retrieved a detailed drawing of streets for the new town. As he began to roll it up, Lillie said, "Those streets don't have names!"

Mr. Ingraham stopped and glanced at her. "Not yet. They will, though."

"You should name them after the flowers and trees around here!" she said, looking like she was ready to show them her favorite drawings again. I suspected she was just looking for another chance to show off her non-alligator drawings.

"You know, that's a good idea," Mr. Ingraham said. He took her drawings back and, leafing quickly through the whole stack, wrote the names of some of her plants next to the streets, including Banyan, Clematis, Datura, Fern, Gardenia, Hibiscus, Iris, Lantana, Myrtle, and Olive, among others.

When he was done, he rolled the plat up and tied it with twine. "Now, don't let this out of your sight until you deliver it personally to the county clerk. For added peace of mind, we'll send one of our boat captains, John Dunn, down there to pick you up. But," he winked at me, "I'm sure you'll be fine. After all, if the federal government trusted you with the mail, I'm sure you can handle this!"

Chapter Eight

The Celestial Railroad

Lillie and I were waiting on the dock the next morning when the *Adelante* steamed into view. It was coming in faster than before, and I soon saw why. Mr. Flagler's regular captain was gone, and instead the boat was captained by a stranger. He seemed to be handling the boat alone, and I had a moment of panic as he barreled toward the dock, then slammed the engine into reverse, and did a tricky sort of turn as he brought the steamer to a stop where we waited.

He stepped out from the cabin, and I got a good look at him. He was short and very broad through the shoulders, with a round belly that strained the buttons of the brown vest he wore over a billowing white shirt. His face was covered in whiskers and he had a long, thin, unlit cigarillo clamped between his teeth.

"Ahoy!" he called to us. His voice was deep and full of laughter. "You must be the Pierce kids. Charlie, I'm guessing," he nodded to me, "and Lillie."

"Yes, sir," I said.

"Nonsense with the sir," he said. "I'm Captain John Dunn aboard my own boat. But aboard Mr. Flagler's pretty little steamer, I'm just Mr. Dunn. A man is only captain of his own ship! Everywhere else he's but an engineer or a deckhand! Now, hop aboard and let's get underway!"

He moved with surprising swiftness for such a large man as he leapt to the rail and lowered the gangplank for Lillie and me to climb onto the *Adelante*. We settled ourselves in the same deck chairs Mama and Papa had sat in as Mr. Dunn went back to the wheelhouse and sent us roaring away from the dock behind a wave of spray.

Lillie and I exchanged a look as Mr. Dunn turned the ship around at full speed and sent us skimming north toward Juno, talking the whole while about his boat *Ethel*—"a small but powerfully fast steamer I ran in Jacksonville"—and how he had been drawn to work for Mr. Flagler, like so many other men. It didn't take long for me to see that Lillie was thoroughly charmed by the brash and rough-and-tumble Mr. Dunn.

The trip up the lake passed in a heartbeat, and soon we came into view of the Juno Courthouse. Juno wasn't much of a village— just the two-story courthouse and a couple of ramshackle wooden buildings huddled on the northern shore of Lake Worth.

But it did have something I was very

interested in seeing, and I strained my ears as the shoreline came into view. Sure enough, a loud shriek shattered the morning silence, and Lillie and I both broke into grins.

"It's the Celestial train!" Lillie exclaimed, running up to the bow to get a better look.

The Celestial Railroad was a narrow-gauge railroad that ran from Jupiter seven and a half miles down to Juno at the top of the lake. The real name of the railroad was the Jupiter & Lake Worth Railway, because it connected Jupiter to the top of Lake Worth, but everybody called it the Celestial Railroad because all the stops were named after Roman gods: Jupiter, Venus, Mars, and Juno.

The train was unusual because it made the return trip to Jupiter going in reverse. There wasn't enough room in the heavy jungle to turn the engine around, so the tracks just ended by the lakeshore. It cost seventy-five cents for a one-way ticket.

We were waving farewell to Mr. Dunn, who said he would wait at the dock for our return trip, when the small steam engine rounded a bend in the track. The engine had a little bulbous smokestack shaped like an onion. It pulled its coal tender and a single passenger car. The train slowed as it passed the courthouse and came to a stop where the track ended. As soon as the engine hissed to a stop, letting out a giant puff of steam, men tumbled off the car. Most of them carried cloth bags, and many of them were black.

"They must be going to work on the hotel," I said.

Lillie nodded. "Lots of new people around here suddenly."

"I guess that's why Flagler wants to build a new town," I answered. "C'mon, let's get these plans delivered."

We headed up the dusty lane to the courthouse. According to Papa, this was one of the most important buildings in the whole area. A few years back, they had moved the county seat of Dade County from down on Biscayne Bay up here to Juno.

Papa said it was because Juno was halfway between the top and bottom of the county, and it made it easier for everyone. Before the county seat moved, people from the lake where we lived had to travel all the way down to Miami to conduct county business. After the election of 1888, however, the people around the lake noticed that more voters lived in the northern end of Dade County than the southern end. They put it to a vote the following year, and the voters agreed to move the county seat from Miami up to Juno. Unfortunately, Papa said, the men in Miami were none too happy about losing the county seat and put up a terrific fight. In the end, Papa said, the men from Lake Worth, including the Dade County Clerk, A.F. Quimby, had to spirit the county records out of Miami at night in a big canoe borrowed from the Seminoles,

through the swamp and then up the coast to Juno.

Looking at the courthouse, it was hard to believe the place had caused so much trouble. The wooden siding was worn gray from the sun and weather, and the windows were dirty with dust and salt. Three sagging steps led up to the front door. We went up together and I pushed the door open, carrying Flagler's plans tucked under my arm.

Inside, it was dim and stuffy. Quimby, the county clerk, had lit a kerosene lantern on the big desk where he sat.

"Why, if it isn't Charlie Pierce," Quimby exclaimed, looking up from his work. "It's nice

to see a face I recognize for once. Seems like all we get through here now are strangers going to work on Mr. Flagler's hotel."

I smiled and said hello while Lillie looked curiously out the window at the men milling around by the lakeshore, waiting for the hotel to send boats to pick them up and take them to work.

"Actually," I said, "that's why I'm here. I'm working for Mr. Flagler too. He asked me to deliver these plans to you."

"So you're a Flagler man now, eh? What plans are these?"

"For a new town for the workers."

74

Quimby nodded. "I'd heard Mr. Flagler was buying land on the west shore of the lake from Captain O.S. Porter and Louie Hillhouse. I heard he paid them forty-five thousand dollars, total, if you can believe it. Couldn't figure out why, though. Thought maybe it was for another hotel."

"It's for a town."

Quimby stretched a hand out and took the roll of paper from me. "You mind?" he asked, not waiting for a reply as he untied the twine and rolled out the paper on his high desk, holding down the edges with an ink pot and one hand. The grid of streets was labeled "Westpalmbeach." The ink had smudged in a few places where Mr. Ingraham had hastily written the street names as Lillie suggested.

"Westpalmbeach," Quimby mused. "Mr. Flagler'll have to run a regular ferry across the lake if he wants to get his men to work every day. Either that or buy a whole fleet of rowboats!" He paused. "I guess that's one more thing that'll change around here. New hotel. New railroad. New town. If I owned the Celestial right about now, I'd be plenty worried."

"What's wrong with the Celestial Railroad?" Lillie demanded, drifting over from the window.

"Oh, nothing," the clerk said. "But it's already expensive to ride it, and sure enough, if Mr. Flagler brings a full-size train all the way down here from Jacksonville, you can bet that

75

little railroad will be out of business before you can say, 'How do you do?'"

Lillie frowned. "That would be terrible. I like the Celestial!"

Quimby laughed. "Oh sure, it was passable enough for a time. But you can't argue with progress, Miss Lillie!"

Lillie grumbled something under her breath as she turned away. I thought I heard the words "progress" and "my foot."

We emerged from the courthouse into the bright sun. The newly arrived men on the shore had all sat down now, scattered under trees and bushes, mopping the sweat away from their faces and necks. They all looked like working men, with rough hands, homemade straw hats, and heavy work clothes. A few of them looked our way and gave us flat stares. When I waved, a handful of men waved back.

Meanwhile, the railroad engineer was busy shoveling coal from a bin into the engine hopper on the Celestial. Soon they would fill the boiler with water for the return trip.

"Charlie," Lillie said. "Can we walk up the street a little? There's a field up there they just cleared. I want to see if I can find something new to draw."

I nodded, and we headed off up the street toward the steaming woods and jungle.

Only a hundred yards north of the lakeshore, the street dwindled into little more than a rutted track with fields of high grass on either side. We pushed up the sandy street, covering a lazy half-mile or so through the big field. Cicadas and grasshoppers screamed in the thick grass, and we saw a thin black snake dozing on the road up ahead. A small tortoise trundled out of the grass, gave us a squinty look, and then headed back into the grass.

"What are we looking for again?" I said.

She was just starting to answer when the little snake raised its head and then suddenly vanished into the grass with a flick of its tail. I was wondering if we had scared it away when the grass parted and a man staggered onto the road. I jumped in surprise and reached out to grab Lillie, but she was already backing away.

It took only a glance to see that the man posed no danger to us. In fact, he was about the sickest, weakest-looking man I'd ever seen. His cheeks were hollow, like he hadn't had a proper meal in weeks, and his clothes hung from him in dirty tatters. Where I could see exposed skin on his shoulders and arms, it was cracked and blistered with a sunburn, and a mosaic of bug bites covered him like stars in a night sky.

He looked up and saw us, and his mouth started to work around a few words. Before he could get them out, three more ghostlike men stumbled from the grass behind him. They all looked the same: starved, sunburned, bug bitten, and red-eyed.

Finally, the first man swallowed hard and croaked out a single word: "Food."

Chapter Nine

The Travelers

"I'm sorry, mister," I said, slowly walking toward the band of ragged men. "I don't have any food with me. But, uh, there's bound to be something back down the road, at the general store."

He swallowed again. "A general store?"

"Are you … are you alright?" I asked. "You all look like you've been dragged through the swamp."

"Two weeks lost in the marsh," he said.

"We're awful hungry," one of the other men chimed in. "You say there's a general store down the way?"

"Sure is," I said. "Follow us. We'll take you to the courthouse. They can help you there."

We turned to head back into Juno, and I took the opportunity to take a good look at the men. I realized the first man who had come out of the brush wasn't too much older than me. The others were all older and looked much worse for the wear.

As we shuffled along, I turned over my shoulder to ask, "So how is it you were in the swamp for two weeks?"

They traded a look amongst themselves, and then the first man said, "We come from Fort Myers. I'm Alfonso Gonzalez. This," he pointed to another man, "is my pal Joe Henley. Them other two are Bill Rew and L. C. Stewart."

"You walked here from Fort Myers?" Lillie butted in. "How'd you get through Pa-Hay-Okee on foot?"

There was a moment of quiet, then Gonzalez said, "We didn't start out walking. We had two canoes. The plan was to head from Fort Myers up to Beautiful Island, camp there, and head out

for Fort Denaud the next morning, then through Lake Hicpochee on the way to Lake Okeechobee. But things started going wrong that first night. We holed up in a palmetto shack on Beautiful Island and woke up the next morning to find the roof of the place was infested with snakes. Must have been three dozen snakes up there, woven through the palmetto."

"What kind of snakes?" I asked.

"We didn't stick around much to find out," the man named Henley pitched in. "We just killed a few and skedaddled."

"True enough," Gonzalez took up the story again. "I have to say, if I never see another snake for the rest of my life, I'll be happy. It wasn't two

"That first day wasn't so bad," Gonzalez said. "The saw grass was five feet or so high, and as long as you didn't brush against it, it wasn't much of a bother. But that soft bottom … you know how it sucks at the feet? Well, Joe here got himself bogged down and soaked his pack with all of our salt. That was the last time I tasted salt in these past two weeks."

"I done told you it wasn't my fault!" Henley said. "That bottom was like quicksand!"

I got the feeling from the general grumbling between the older men they'd had this conversation plenty of times before.

"After that it was just one problem piled on another," Gonzalez said. "We found ourselves

days later that a water moccasin tried to take a fresh-killed turkey right out of my hands. That snake was six feet if he was an inch. Instead of fighting him, I lopped the head off the turkey and let Mr. Snake have it."

Lillie and I grinned.

"The next day we sailed across the lake in our canoes, heading for Pelican Island, and camped there for the night," Gonzalez continued. "The mosquitoes were so bad that night I thought they might lift one of us up and carry us away. We camped there, then the next morning left the canoes on the shore and headed out on foot across the swamp."

"That's hard traveling," I said.

in a stream filled with water moccasins chasing minnows. Rew had to clear the way through the snakes with his gun barrel. Then L.C. went into the muck and lost his shoes, so he was wading barefoot. We spent almost six hours going a single mile and we'd had two men half-buried in muck, contended with a river of snakes, and lost all of our salt.

"From there, it only got worse. There was no dry land to speak of, just that infernal plain of saw grass, muck, and water. What little dry land existed was so choked with vines and rusty old trees, so infested with insects, that it was little better than being knee-deep in the muck. We ended up getting plenty lost, and pretty soon we ran out of food, so had to eat cabbage palm hearts. They wasn't so bad at first, but after a week solid of nothing else but cabbage heart with no salt, I would almost rather have eaten sand. I tell you, there were times that it wasn't a certain thing all of us would live through that trip."

"Oh my," Lillie said. "Why did you leave your canoes behind?"

"Figured it would be easier to walk," Gonzalez said. "We thought the whole trip through the swamp would take four days. Not ten. I'd say next time we'll do it different, but there won't be a next time as far as I'm concerned."

The other men nodded glumly in agreement. Up ahead, I could see the road widening as we neared the courthouse.

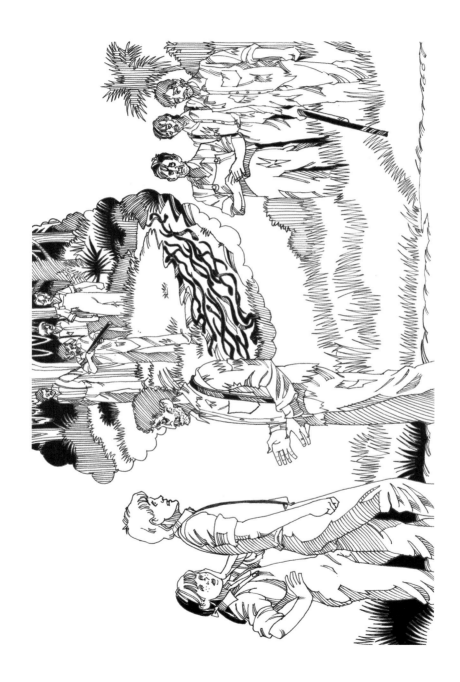

"So why'd you come over here in the first place?" Lillie said. "What's over here that's worth risking your neck over?"

Bill Rew gave a short laugh. "Henry Flagler, that's what."

"Henry Flagler?" I said, then it hit me. "Oh. You're looking for work."

"That's right," Gonzalez said. "Between Flagler's railroad and hotel, and the canal project we heard so much about, all the action is over here now. Once we get some food and decent sleep, we'll see about signing on."

Just then, we rounded a corner and the first rickety building came into view. The courthouse loomed over the dusty street, and beyond that the lake glittered in the afternoon sun. The men picked up their pace, heading toward the little general store and hopefully to food, rest, and shelter.

Personally, I considered it a miracle that none of them had died on the trip over, whether from animals or exposure to the elements. Surely the great Pa-Hay-Okee had swallowed up men with more outdoor experience than these. But somehow these men had survived on foot through snake- and gator-infested swamplands to come here and work on Henry Flagler's dream of a hotel.

Until now, I'd felt the pull of Mr. Flagler's words myself, his vision of well-groomed ladies and men promenading in front of a gabled building that gleamed in the sun, of guests being pedaled along my Jungle Trail to see exotic plants and animals. But this was the first time I really understood what Flagler's vision could do to men. It was so strong that it called to men from all over the state to risk their lives to be part of it. Papa and Lillie might not approve of the changes it brought, but the sight of these four ragged men, more than anything else so far, convinced me that change was coming. None of us knew what would be on the other side of that change.

Just then, a lonely whistle sounded above the trees, as if in response to my thoughts. It was the Celestial Railroad, finally refueled with coal, driving backward out of Juno and heading back up north to get another load of men coming down to change South Florida forever.

Chapter Ten

A Flagler Man

The next few months passed quickly. There was more work than could be done, and I collapsed into my bed every night, exhausted. During the day, there were chores around the farm. When I wasn't in the fields, planting and tending the fall crops, I was sailing up the lake to the hotel, where Mr. McDonald had me doing all manner of tasks. Sometimes I ran messages. Sometimes I swung a hammer. And sometimes I worked with Haley Mickens to help prepare the Jungle Trail and build the sheds where the pedaled carts would be stored

when they finally arrived from the factory up north.

When it came to the Jungle Trail, Mickens wanted everything to be perfect. "This is my first real job, Charlie," he'd say, grinning. "Everything's got to be just right, so Mr. Flagler sees he made the right choice. I'm gonna run the best concession anywhere in Mr. Flagler's empire!"

As the summer days drained away into fall and then into the Christmas season, the urgency at the hotel picked up. Without the heat and rain of summer, the men worked harder and longer than ever before. And there were more of them. The Styx had grown up quickly into a fair-sized town, its dusty streets lined with all manner of shacks. The working men had built everything from crude huts thrown together from a few palm fronds to solid wooden buildings with shingled roofs and little chimneys that puffed smoke.

I wondered who was tending those fires—for there were few women in The Styx and the men mostly worked at the hotel site. I knew from spending time in The Styx that these men had come from all over. They were the children of freed slaves, and some were freed slaves themselves. Others had come from the Caribbean. Just as it was for Gonzalez and his

friends, Flagler's hotel was a powerful lure for men of all types to come looking for good work.

But it seemed like lonely and hard work.

I asked Mama about it one afternoon, and she set down the dish she was washing and stared at me for a full minute before she answered. "Why, Charlie, you're right. I suppose I never thought of that either! What kind of neighbors would we be if we just left those men up there without doing what we could to help them!"

From that day on, I'd leave the house and head for the boat only to have Mama chase after me, calling, "Charlie! Wait! Take this with you!" And she'd have a basket full of warm muffins or little cakes or fresh fruit. Sometimes she'd put in jars of sea grape or guava jelly that had been sealed with wax. Once she included a bundle of dried venison jerky from last season, wrapped in a sheet of burlap and tied with twine.

It didn't take long for the men of The Styx to realize that when I showed up with a basket, good things were about to happen. The cry would go up, "Ho! It's Charlie Pierce with a basket of his mama's cooking!" and the streets would fill up with hopeful men looking for some home cooking.

The hotel project, meanwhile, had moved inside. The skeleton of the building had been covered with wood sheets, and the roofing crew was putting on shingles. Now, the vast building swallowed several hundred men every morning like a tremendous ant hill, the men trooping through the big doors in a line carrying their tools and supplies. All day, the sound of work echoed over the water as men swarmed in and around the hotel. Everywhere, the men talked about finishing first, "before them train boys can get down here."

I figured they probably would. Last I'd heard, Papa said the train would reach Fort Pierce in January before it could make the final push down to Lake Worth. The hotel team were sure they would finish before the first train rolled down to the lake. From what Mr. Ingraham said, the hotel would be ready to open by February.

***

On a cool December afternoon, I was

tending the winter vegetable garden and thinking about what the hotel would look like when it was done when Papa came to stand at the edge of the garden plot. He had his hands on his hips and his big straw hat pushed way back on his head so he could look at the sky.

"Hi, Papa," I said, straightening up and wiping the dirt from my hands. "Everything alright?"

"Hmm," he said. "I don't know, Charlie. What do you think? Awful still this afternoon, isn't it? Wouldn't mind seeing some clouds myself."

"Clouds?"

"Mmm hmm," he said. "Clouds are like a blanket. They keep the heat in. A still, clear day like this. I'm thinking tonight'll be a cold one."

"You think we'll have to get out the pots and cover up?"

"Maybe," he said. "We'll keep an eye on it as the sun goes down."

From that moment, the temperature started dropping fast. With just a few hours of light left in the day, Papa came back to the garden and said, "Alright, Charlie. Let's cover up."

Lillie appeared outside, her cheeks red from the cold and excitement. I'd seen snow when I was little, back in Chicago, but Lillie had been born here and had never seen more than a little frost.

Still, even a little frost was too much for Papa. Our winter vegetable garden was full of tomatoes, peppers, and corn. A freeze would kill everything. This wasn't even to mention the pineapples, coconuts, and other fruits from warmer places.

"C'mon, Lillie. You can help us," Papa said, blowing into his hands and heading for the outbuilding where we kept great rolls of burlap row covers and the smudge pots.

For the next hour or so, we worked hard to protect our crops. First we watered everything real deep, dumping buckets of water between the rows. Papa said the extra water in the soil would protect the roots and help keep them warm. While I was lugging the pails of water back and forth, Lillie built a small wood fire and then knocked it down so we'd have a good bed of coals. Next we shoveled a tiny pile of coals into each of our round smudge pots and then hurried with the hot little pots to the garden to place them between the rows. The pots had holes in them to let smoke escape, and pretty soon the garden was full of smoking globes. Finally, we unrolled the burlap and tented it over the plants. As we covered the garden, the tents filled with warm smoke that would protect the plants through the long, cold night.

By this time, my hands were raw and near frozen. Papa kept blowing on his hands to warm them, stopping only to stare at the fields of pineapples. "We've got to water them in good," he said. "Fill up their cups with just as much water as we can and hope."

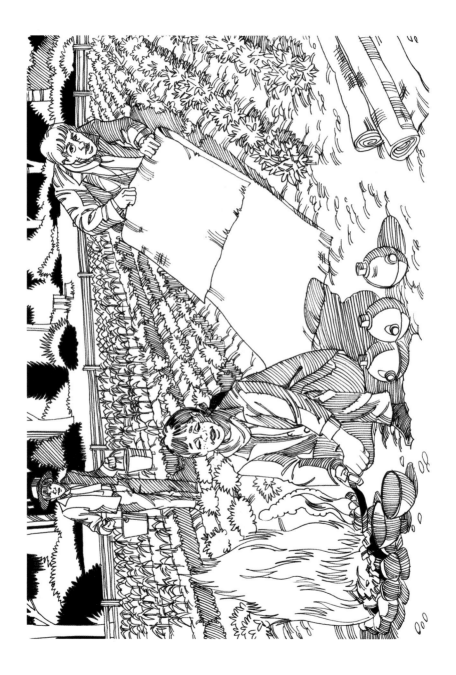

Trudging back to get more water for the pineapples, I pictured the long rows of spiky plants all covered in frost and hoped they'd be okay. Then a new picture hopped into my mind: the rows of vegetables in gardens throughout The Styx. I knew from my time there that most of the men had gardens behind their shacks. From what I could tell, they shared gardening work, so whenever a man had some time off, he'd help tend to all the gardens. This way, the men had access to fresh food, plus whatever they could hunt. Without their own gardens and hunting, there'd never be enough to feed all the men working on the hotel.

I set the bucket down and turned back to find Papa. He was staking down the smoky burlap over our own vegetables. He looked up as I approached.

"Where's your bucket, Charlie? Don't tell me it sprung a leak."

"No, Papa. But … I just realized. I've got to go. I've got to sail up the lake to help the men at the hotel and The Styx to protect their crops too."

Papa straightened up and blew on his hands. "Charlie, it's late afternoon. It'll be near dark by the time you get up there. And anyway, we still need to water the pineapples in."

"Lillie can handle that, Papa. I know it's late, but … the men up there don't know it's going to freeze tonight. They're not from here. They don't know what to do. They'll be ruined!"

"Charlie, listen, I respect your wanting to

help them. But this isn't your problem. We have work here that needs doing."

"But, Papa, they'll lose their food."

"I'm sorry if that happens, Charlie. But you don't know that for certain. For all you know, they're already covering up. And besides, can't Mr. Flagler just ship down whatever he wants? Seems like this is a Mr. Flagler problem, not a Charlie Pierce problem."

"If this was any other new neighbor, you'd want me to go!"

Papa frowned and looked surprised. "Now, what's that supposed to mean?"

"You're just not letting me go because it's the hotel and you don't like the hotel. If it was any other neighbor, you'd make me go even if I didn't want to."

"Well, that's true for neighbors, Charlie, but you can hardly call that hotel a neighbor!"

"Why not, Papa? Why aren't they neighbors we should help?"

"Well, because ... it's just ... oh, for the devil, Charlie, Mr. Flagler is a millionaire many times over! He doesn't need our help to do much of anything as far as I can see. He's just going to do whatever his money lets him do."

"Papa, that's not fair. Those men up there aren't millionaires. They're just men who work on the hotel. And besides, Mr. Flagler isn't doing anything wrong! That hotel will be good for us here. You should see the way the men love Mama's cooking. Why, I bet she could start a business selling her jam and make a nice profit. And Lillie … what if she wins that drawing contest? That would be fifty dollars!"

Papa looked at me for a few seconds without speaking, slowly shaking his head. "Listen to yourself, Charlie. You've got Mama going into business for herself. Lillie winning a contest. And Mr. Flagler is the white knight coming to make everything better. Has it crossed your mind that there's a reason we're seeing less game in the woods? That you bring enough men down here and the fish will soon disappear? Heck, Charlie, you know they're digging a canal in addition to that new railroad. Where do you think that canal is going to run when it gets here? I'll tell you where. Right into our lake, Charlie. Right into our lake."

"So? Who cares if there's a canal?" I replied angrily.

"I care, and so should every family living here," Papa answered.

"You just don't like Mr. Flagler," I said.

Papa shook his head wearily. "No, Charlie. That ain't it at all. I don't know Mr. Flagler. He seems like a nice enough gentleman. My concern is that people are talking about making big changes to the land, our land, and I don't see anybody asking if all this is a good idea. I don't see anybody wondering what a hotel, a train, and a canal, not to mention thousands of visitors from up north, will do to the woods, the lake and streams. Do you know, Charlie?"

I hung my head and kicked at the dirt. Quimby's words "So you're a Flagler man now" bubbled up in my mind. I looked up defiantly. "This is progress, Papa. And far as I can see, you're the only one against it."

"He ain't the only one," Lillie said. She had come to hear what we were arguing about. I shot her a "shut your mouth" look but waited to see what Papa would say.

Papa took a deep breath and puffed it out. It was cold enough now that his breath fogged out of his mouth in a cloud of steam like a dragon.

"I don't know that you've got the right of this," Papa said. "I think you're having trouble separating out what could be done from what should be done." I started to object, but he raised his hand to silence me. "But you're not the only one having that problem, Charlie, and you're right about one thing. If we had a new neighbor up the lake who needed help, I'd see to it that we helped them if we could. So go on. If you want to get up the lake, you better leave now. And be careful, Charlie. We don't know how cold it's going to get before dawn."

Chapter Eleven

Growing Pains

There was hardly a puff of wind in the cold, clear air, but I sailed as fast as I could. When I did finally arrive at the place where I usually tied up, the brightest stars were twinkling overhead. The cold seemed to sharpen the stars.

I had to jump off the boat into lake water, which felt warm compared to the air, and headed at a run straight for The Styx and Haley Mickens's house. He lived alone in a tiny shack with a crooked chimney and one cracked, lopsided window he'd scavenged from the hotel. I knocked on his door, hoping he was home.

"Charlie?" he said, opening the door a crack and looking surprised. "What are you doing pounding on my door and looking like you done ran all the way here? You need to come inside before I lose all my warm air."

"Haley," I said, panting. "You need to get some men together. To protect your crops. It's going to freeze tonight."

Haley looked up at the sky. "Freeze? It don't freeze here!"

"It does," I said. "Not often, but it does. It'll kill everything in the ground if we don't do something fast!"

Haley quickly grabbed a jacket and came with me. We ran from door to door to rustle up a group of men, then we went hunting for material. We needed as much burlap as we could find, plus clay or metal pots, and buckets of warm water.

I gathered some of the men around me and showed them how to make row covers from burlap, then how to put just a few hot coals into the pots and bury them neck-deep between their rows of vegetables. In the meantime, a steady stream of men trooped into the plots of vegetables with buckets of water, soaking down the soil before we covered the rows.

We worked hard and fast, starting with the biggest vegetable gardens. As we worked, the temperature continued to drop steadily.

Soon it was completely dark and colder than I could ever remember. At one point, I looked up to see a white man standing in the road watching us. He was one of the foremen from the hotel, but I didn't know his name. We exchanged a wave, then he turned and headed back down the road.

The moon had fully risen and we didn't finish

the last garden until midnight. All over The Styx, vegetable gardens huddled under their burlap blankets, the plants bathed in warm smoke.

"I hope it's enough," I said.

"Yes sir, me too," Haley answered. "And thank you, Charlie. I expect a lot of men here will be grateful to you tomorrow morning."

"It's no problem," I said. "That's what neighbors do."

We said our good-byes and I walked back down the trail to the hotel. The job site was complete empty. It was strange to walk around the bulk of the giant, deserted building. It felt like the hotel was staring down at me through the thousand empty eyes of its windows. I hurried to the shore to my boat, then stopped and looked across the lake.

The surface of the water was flat like a sheet of hammered tin. It glowed brightly in the moonlight. There were no night birds singing, no bats swooping over the water. The world was as still and quiet as I could ever remember, and for a second I imagined that I was the last person left on a cold and glittering Earth.

I shook my head to clear it and wondered what I should do next. There was no way I could sail down the lake to go home. There was no wind at all. I looked around, thinking.

I considered sneaking into the empty hotel

for the night, but a chill ran up my spine when I imagined spending the night alone in the huge, deserted hotel. I could go back to Haley's shack, but I knew he didn't have any room for me. I'd be sleeping on the cold dirt.

Then my eye caught the construction shack. It had a raised wood floor, a potbellied iron stove, and benches. It would have to do.

I walked to the shack and reached for the door, breathing a sigh of relief when it opened up and I let myself into the dark. The shack smelled of old cigar smoke, lamp oil, and paper. Before long I had a cheery little fire going in the iron stove and a kerosene lamp throwing light onto the scene.

Careful not to disturb any of the papers, I stretched out on a wood bench, blew out the lamp, and closed my eyes to sleep, grateful for the heat radiating from the stove.

***

"My oh my, look what we've got here."

My eyes flew open and, for one second, I had no idea where I was or who was talking. It didn't sound like Papa, but who else did I know with a deep voice?

Then I remembered: I had slept the night in the construction shack by the hotel. The fire had gone cold, and the room was icy. Light flooded in the windows and the open front door, where none other than Mr. McDonald and Mr. Flagler stood in the doorway. They were wrapped in heavy coats and staring at me.

I sat up groggily. "Uh, I'm, ah, I'm sorry, sir. I got stranded—"

"We were just wondering whose work that was in the vegetable gardens up in The Styx," Mr. McDonald said. "Looks like we've got our answer, wouldn't you say, sir?"

"Looks like," Flagler answered. "What say you, Charlie Pierce? Was that you working with the men last evening to protect their gardens?"

"Yes, sir. I, uh, I was afraid they would lose their crops. I couldn't let that happen."

"And good thing you didn't," Flagler said. "Fact is, you just saved all their fresh food." He came into the room, taking off his jacket while Mr. McDonald headed toward the stove to light it up for the day. Flagler hung his jacket on a coat rack and sat down in one of the chairs, putting his hands on his knees and looking at me from beneath his bushy eyebrows.

"I owe you another thank-you, young man," Flagler said. "Here's the thing about leading an enterprise like this. You learn over time that your main job isn't putting up hotels or building railways. It's taking care of your people, so they can build the hotels and lay the rails. When you help me take care of my men the way you did last night, you help me in the most profound way possible."

"Thank you, sir," I said, pride welling in my chest. Then I remembered the fight I'd had with

Papa the night before. "I wish my Papa felt the same way."

"Yes, I know your papa's not too happy about my hotel," Flagler said. "But ... you ever had a growing pain, Charlie? You know what that is?"

I nodded.

"It's like this. When your bones are growing, it can hurt something awful. I remember it from my own boyhood, like an ache in your legs. But when that growing pain goes away, what's left? Why, you've grown another inch or two! And that's just what it's often like with people like your papa. It hurts to grow, to change. But when we're done here, why Charlie, there won't be a man on this continent who could stand before the hotel we're building and not feel awe."

"I hope so, sir. He was pretty upset at me for coming up here."

Flagler nodded. "I'll tell you what, Charlie. Here's what we'll do. Considering you've now helped me three times, I'd like to do something for you and your family. I'd like for your family to attend the hotel's grand opening as my personal guests."

I had never thought of this before. In truth, I had no idea what a grand opening even meant. "Thank you, sir, but ... I'm afraid I don't know what to do at a grand opening."

Flagler smiled. "Just as well! You don't have to worry about anything but enjoying yourself. Now, tell me. Do you have a proper suit, Charlie?"

"A suit? No, sir."

Flagler stood up. "We'll take care of everything, then. You just run along home now and tell your papa and mama that they are invited, and that I personally insist on them coming. We'll see then what your papa says about growing pains."

I recognized he was dismissing me, so I stood up and stretched, heading for the door. Mr. Flagler and Mr. McDonald followed me. When I stepped outside, I stopped in shock. It was bitterly cold, and everywhere I looked, the ground and plants were covered with a fine sparkling blanket of frost. The cold pulled at my cheeks and lips. It didn't look like my home at all, but some other strange landscape straight from a fairy tale.

I headed down the steps and toward my boat.

"Now, remember when you get home to pass along my invitation," Flagler called after me. "And be on the lookout for a surprise."

Chapter Twelve

Top Hats and Tails

Mr. Flagler was awful confident that Papa would come around, but I wasn't so sure. Fact is, I knew Papa wasn't some backwoods farmer who had never seen civilization and would be bowled over by the sight of a big hotel. Papa had lived in Chicago, sailed around the world, visited Australia and Papua New Guinea, and even sailed around Cape Horn at the bottom of South America.

The way he told it, he and Mama moved to the jungles of South Florida because it was full of opportunity—even if it was a hard life. Papa liked the wide open spaces, the wild animals, and the empty beaches. I didn't know if there was anything Mr. Flagler could say that would change Papa's mind on that, no matter how grand his hotel was.

It was still early afternoon when I reached our island and tied up to the dock. The temperature was rising as the sun came up, and I found Papa and Lillie in the fields and gardens, pulling up the burlap, packing away the pots, and snipping away browned and frozen leaves.

"Papa," I said, approaching him as he knelt over a row of pineapples and removed brown leaves.

"Charlie," he said. "What happened to you last night?"

"We didn't finish till very late and there wasn't enough wind to sail home, so I slept up there. How are the crops?"

Papa looked over the fields. "All in all, I'd say it could have been much worse. Lost some pineapples and some vegetables, but most of it came through alright." He paused. "How'd it go up there?"

"I think okay," I said. "We covered up as many gardens as we could. And, uh, this morning Mr. Flagler stopped in, I think to see if the freeze hurt anything. And," I paused, "he invited us to the hotel's grand opening."

Papa gave me a quizzical look. "He did, did he? And what do you think, Charlie? You think we ought to go?"

"I think we should," I said. Then I quickly added, "It would be the neighborly thing to do."

Papa smiled at me. "Well, then, I guess we'll see what all the fuss is about. Now, why don't you give me a hand here and let's see about getting these pineapples back in shape."

***

Christmas came and went, then New Year's, and we settled into a breezy and cool South

105

Florida winter that gave way to a warm spring. Now that the Jungle Trail was finished, I didn't go up to the hotel much anymore. I missed Haley Mickens and the other men of The Styx. I missed the hotel too—I wondered what the men were doing now and what the grounds looked like.

As if he knew I was feeling restless, Papa kept me extra busy in the fields, so I was busy working in the spring vegetable garden one morning when I heard a familiar whistle pierce the air. I looked up the lake to see the *Adelante* chugging toward us. The rest of the family joined me, and we waited by the dock as Captain John Dunn once again expertly docked the steamer.

We were soon greeted by the cheerful voice of Haley Mickens. He was leaning against the bow railing and waving to us with his hat.

"Nice to meet you, Mr. and Mrs. Pierce!" he called. "Hey, Charlie!"

A group of men emerged from the cabin and, led by Haley, trooped down the gangplank onto the dock. Papa looked thoroughly confused, but Mama quickly offered them all some coffee.

"No, thank you, ma'am," Haley said. "We're just here to make a delivery. If you don't mind, do you have someplace dry we could leave a few crates?"

"Crates?" Papa echoed. "Crates of what?"

"I don't rightly know," Haley said. "I just know I'm supposed to deliver them to you."

Papa showed the men into our house. They looked doubtfully at the small space. I soon understood why as they went back to the steamer and carried two large wooden crates off the boat. The crates were big enough that each needed two men to carry it. The men left the crates in the middle of our house, and then bade us good-bye and boarded the boat to leave.

Alone, we stood around the two crates, all of us equally puzzled. They were both stamped "NEW YORK CITY" in big black letters, and

Mama's eyes shined at the mention of the big city. "I wonder what it is," she breathed.

"Lillie," Papa said, "will you go fetch my hammer and crowbar? Let's see what this is all about."

Mama, Lillie, and I watched in fascination as Papa pried the top off the first crate to reveal densely packed straw. He dug both arms into the straw, sneezing as the chaff drifted into his nose, and then withdrew a carefully wrapped package. He slit it open and lifted up a full-length lace and velvet gown of the deepest blue.

"What the—"

"Why, that's a ball gown!" Mama

interrupted, brushing her hands against the soft fabric. "My goodness! Oh, Papa! Feel this fabric! It's soft as a cloud!"

As Mama grabbed the dress and held it up against her shoulders, muttering about taking in a little here, letting out a little there, Papa dug back into the crate and emerged with another carefully wrapped package. He slit this one open and held up another, smaller dress. It was pure white with a light purple ribbon at the waist and tiny beads glittering in the neckline.

"I am not wearing that," Lillie said flatly, and I couldn't help it, but I burst into laughter at the thought of my rough-and-tumble tomboy little sister dressed up in a lacy gown.

"Oh, Lillie!" Mama exclaimed when she saw the dress. She set her own gown down and snatched the dress from Papa's hands. "You're going to look like an angel, honey! We'll do your hair up. My goodness!"

As she spoke she was trying to hold the dress up to Lillie's shoulders, but Lillie was too quick for her and kept slipping away.

I was laughing so hard I had to hold my sides to keep from splitting while Lillie shot me poisonous looks and tried to escape from Mama. But Papa soon cut across my laughter. "There's another crate, Charlie. What do you want to bet …?" He let it trail off, and suddenly I realized what he meant.

Sure enough, the second crate held two formal suits. And they weren't just any suits, made from homespun cloth with carved buttons like our clothes. These were black waistcoats—at least that's what Papa called the vests—and formal tailcoats that hung to the backs of my knees. There were two snowy white shirts, plus shiny shoes, and some type of fabric strip that Mama told me was a bow tie, although I had no earthly idea how that was possible, because it had no shape. And worst of all, there were two tall and glossy top hats.

Papa put one on my head and one on his own head, tilting it back as he laughed and declared, "Don't you worry about that bow tie, Charlie! I'll show you how it's done." Then it was Lillie's turn to laugh as Papa grabbed Mama

and they twirled around our living room for a few turns.

"Oh Lord, help me," Mama said, grinning. "I'm almost forgetting myself!"

I had no idea what she meant, but then, watching my parents dance for the first time in my life, I think I understood. It was easy to forget the fields, the hard work, the steaming jungle, when the house smelled of straw and fine clothes from New York City, when Mama and Papa both wore faraway looks like they were in some other building in a different place and time.

Once again, I felt that familiar sensation of wonder at the change wrought by Mr. Flagler. It was like he had reached deep into my family

and sprinkled this moment with magic dust. Even Lillie—who was careful not to get too close to her own dress, as if it might bite her—looked happily on as Mama and Papa danced.

When they were done, Papa dug back into the crate and removed the final item: a large and sturdy envelope with formal curly writing on the front: "The Pierce Family."

He opened it and slid a card out, and then read it aloud: "You are cordially invited to the Grand Opening of the Hotel Royal Poinciana, courtesy of Mr. Henry Flagler."

It was followed by a date barely a week away.

Papa set the card down and took the top hat off his head. "Well, I guess the deed is done," he said, and the glowing look from just a minute before slipped off his face like an outgoing tide.

"Oh, don't fuss," Mama said, still grinning. "This is the beginning of a new day!"

A slight frown crossed Papa's face, and when he said, "I suppose it is," I wasn't sure he was all that happy about it.

Chapter Thirteen

Into a New World

The day of the party approached quickly, and it was fun watching Mama's excitement grow with every passing day. She tried her dress on every day while she was sewing it to fit just right. Mama tried a few times to get Lillie to try her dress on, but Lillie found a way to vanish every time Mama started talking about the party. One day Lillie actually covered herself with mud so she'd be too dirty to touch the white dress.

On the day of the party, all four of us took baths and got dressed in our finery. When I glanced at myself in our small mirror, I almost didn't recognize the boy looking back at me. He was wearing a waistcoat and tailcoat with a shiny hat and the bow tie Papa had helped tie in a complicated knot. His blonde hair was neatly combed and parted and his face was scrubbed clean.

We headed for the hotel in the late afternoon. Even from a distance, I could feel the excitement in the air. The train tracks had finally arrived in the new town of Westpalmbeach, and a rail terminal had been built on the west shore of the lake.

I remembered delivering the plans for the town to Quimby up in Juno. Back then, the lakeshore was still open fields and forest. Now, a full-sized steam engine sat idling alongside the new terminal, a trail of steam rising from its smokestack. This gleaming black engine was big enough to swallow the Celestial steam engine whole, and it pulled an entire line of rail cars. I could see these were private luxury cars. I heard Mama catch her breath.

A steady stream of boats was already crossing the lake, heading toward the hotel. The boats were brand new and painted white. Each boat had a lantern in the bow, and the passengers were seated in rows while they gazed at the hotel.

And the hotel itself! It was my turn to gasp as it came into view.

A broad avenue lined with huge palm trees ran from the lakeshore to the front entrance. The entire six-story structure was painted a light yellow with white trim and green shutters. A large covered veranda ran along the front of the hotel, facing the lake behind rows of tall columns. Hundreds of windows glittered along the face of the building, and the tower high above the entrance was topped with an American flag that snapped in the breeze.

"Good Lord," Papa said. "I … I … hardly know what to think."

"It's huge," Lillie said, her aggravation over her dress forgotten and her eyes wide.

"Right there," I said, pointing to the dense woods just south of the hotel. "That's where my Jungle Trail is. I'll show you when we get there."

We approached the new dock. A man dressed in a fine white uniform waited on us at the dock. I didn't recognize him, but I figured he most likely lived in The Styx and was new to the area.

"Welcome to the Hotel Royal Poinciana!" he called, holding his hand out for a rope to tie us up. "Please proceed to the entrance and present your invitation!"

We climbed from our boat and walked along the avenue toward the hotel. The building seemed to grow as we approached, until I could hardly see the top of the flag even with my head craned all the way back. Men in tailcoats and women in fancy gowns and dripping with jewels joined us on the path, all of them talking about how fine the hotel was.

More attendants stood at the front doors. I looked around for anyone I recognized as they took our invitation, but all I saw were strange faces. No Haley Mickens. No James Ingraham. No neighbors. And no Henry Flagler.

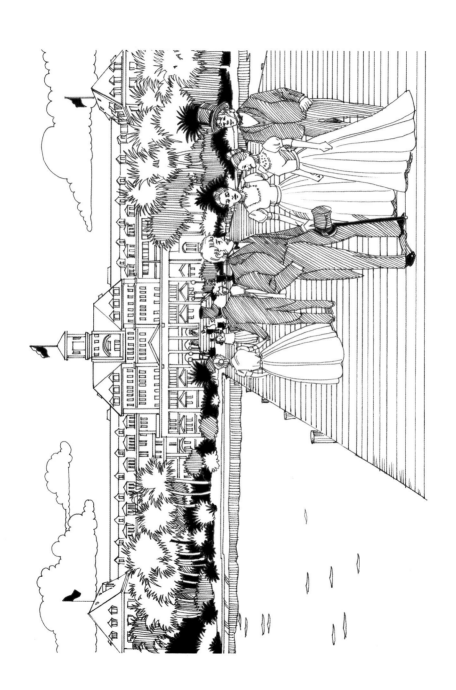

"If you would follow me," one of the attendants said. "We're just about to start a regular tour of the building for Mr. Flagler's guests. I'll be happy to show you the most remarkable aspects of this magnificent hotel."

We fell in with the guide without a word between us, and I had the sense we were all being swept along in a current that was too strong to resist. He led us down a short hall and up a flight of stairs into a large and beautiful room he called the Rotunda. Clusters of chairs were gathered around the room's many columns. Hallways and curving stairs led off in every direction. A dome reached up into the upper floors.

Our guide headed down one of the halls,

his words floating ahead of us. "The sheer size of the hotel is staggering," he said, "especially considering there was nothing but wasteland here before Mr. Flagler arrived." I saw Papa scowl and exchange a glance with Lillie.

"Within this one building," the guide continued, "there are five hundred and forty individual guest rooms, each decorated with the finest appointments and available at nightly rates from six dollars to one hundred dollars. There are three miles of hallways leading to salons, a library and reading room, parlors, drawing rooms, and the dining room. No detail has been overlooked. No expense has been spared. We even have electric lights!"

As he talked, we followed him through a maze of rooms and halls.

"Already," the guide was saying, "interest in the hotel is so strong that Mr. Flagler is laying plans to expand the structure to add more guest rooms. People from all over the world—royalty, leading industrialists, heads of state—have expressed an interest in coming here to see this extraordinary building."

I glanced at Papa and his scowl deepened.

"And now," the guide said with a flourish, stopping before a set of double doors, "the final stop on our tour: the dining room." He bowed and waved us into an immense room. "Welcome to the Hotel Royal Poinciana."

We joined the stream of high-society people passing into the dining room. At one end

of the room there was a bandstand where a band played classical music that floated above the crowd. Large round tables set with white tablecloths and more silver than I had ever seen were arranged throughout, with waiters in white uniforms moving among them.

"Oh my," Mama said, her eyes shining. "Papa, isn't this something! A ball! Lillie, you'll dance your first dance tonight!"

"Humph," Lillie said. "I'd rather not."

Mama didn't hear her as she grabbed Papa's hand and led him away from us, toward the dance floor, weaving through the crowd.

Lillie and I stood in astonishment and

117

watched our parents dance as the sunlight faded and the room was lit with the flicker of a hundred lamps. The dancing crowd seemed to move faster as the hour grew later, people whirling and laughing. Waiters carried trays of fine hors d'oeuvres and drinks. The hall was filled with the clatter of hundreds of people talking at once, and I wondered how any kitchen could possibly feed all these people at once.

I felt a hand on my arm and saw Lillie looking up at me.

"If we stay here too much longer, Mama's gonna make us dance, Charlie," she said. "Show me your Jungle Trail, would you? I can't be in this noise too much longer. It's making my head hurt."

I shook my head to clear it. "Okay. C'mon."

It was dusk when we stepped outside, crossed the veranda, and headed down the path that led through the grounds. Lillie stopped every so often to examine and exclaim over the plants on the property. Even the landscaping was like nothing I'd ever seen. There were graceful coconut palms waving in the breeze. Fruit trees bearing all types of strange fruits. Bushes and shrubs with red leaves or strange hanging flowers like trumpets, plants that must have traveled a thousand miles from the jungles of South America or Asia to find themselves here. Lillie pointed at a great umbrella-shaped tree.

"That's a Royal Poinciana tree," she said.

"They're from Madagascar. I've never seen one in real life."

"That's the tree the hotel is named after," I said.

We went on until we reached the very barn I'd helped build months before. It had been painted the same pale yellow as the hotel and was surrounded by a crowd of people, all talking and waiting in line. I recognized Haley Mickens's voice and saw him up front, helping ladies onto the special wheeled carts for tours of the Jungle Trail. I hoped to catch his eye, but he was busy, so we waited in line.

"Charlie!" he said when we reached the front of the line. "Hey! Step right up and get yourself

a ride through the exotic jungle!" As he led us to a cart, he whispered to me, "What did I tell you? Best concession in the South!"

I laughed as we climbed into a strange-looking bicycle contraption with a wicker chair up front and a regular bike seat and pedals in the back. One of the workers from The Styx sat behind us. He started to pedal as soon as we were seated. He kept up a steady stream of chatter about the hotel and its grounds.

Even though I had helped build the trail, I hardly recognized it. Torches attached to the trees lit the way, making shadows dance in the jungle, and the forest floor had been planted with more exotic palms and bushes. It looked

119

like another place, and I half expected to see monkeys flitting through the trees.

Coming back from the tour was like stepping back into my normal world.

"So?" Haley said as we said our good-byes. "What'd you think?"

"It's ... incredible," I said. "It doesn't look anything like the jungle we started with!"

"No sir," Haley said, grinning. "I reckon this will be the most popular attraction at the whole hotel!"

I didn't know if that was true, but I hoped so for Haley's sake as we wandered back through the gardens to the hotel. Back in the dining room, the party was still in full swing as Lillie said, "I'm hungry. When do you think they'll serve dinner?"

"I don't know," I said. "I'll see if I can go find out."

I left Lillie sitting alone at one of the big round tables, swinging her foot from the chair and sipping a glass of lemonade. I wasn't sure what I was looking for exactly, but I knew I wanted to be with my own thoughts for a minute. I hadn't known what to expect, but this ... Everything was bigger, grander, stranger, and louder than I'd imagined. I hadn't expected the crowds, the glittering men and women wrapping their mouths around strange words in accents from New York and Boston. They talked about stocks and speculation, mineral rights, stockyards, Monte Carlo in the summer ... a foreign world that rang in my ears in bits of sentences and made me feel itchy in my strange suit, awkward and uncomfortable.

I wished I could find Mr. Flagler. I felt like he could settle me, help me feel more comfortable in this overwhelming place.

Instead, I found my Papa.

Chapter Fourteen

A Rare Man

He was standing alone near the dance floor with his hat in his hands. I didn't see Mama anywhere. My first thought was to talk to Papa, but something about the way he was standing, the way his shoulders were slumped, made me stay back. He looked like he needed a minute with his own thoughts too.

Then I heard the men talking.

There were four of them standing in a group and talking to each other. I didn't recognize them but could tell from their accents they were from up north. They all wore tailcoats and top hats, like us, and they had big moustaches and furry sideburns growing down their cheeks. Unlike us, they looked as comfortable in their formal clothes as I would in my overalls, like they wore tails every day of the week.

"Absolutely," one of them was saying. "You'd be a fool not to see it."

The others nodded.

"They say this place was nothing but alligators and snakes until Henry found it," a second man added. "But now that he's got a railroad here …" He let it trail off as a third man picked up the thread: "It's almost too late to get in on the ground floor. You mark my words, there's going to be a land rush here. It'll be bigger than the gold rush of forty-eight. I hear that some pieces of land are already going for tens of thousands."

The men all laughed knowingly.

"The key will be finding the right pieces of property, and then hiding your hand as you move in," another one threw in. "I understand most of the land around here is owned by local farmers. They use it to grow pineapples and vegetables. They have no idea what they're sitting on. Pick it up for pennies, sell it for dollars, I say."

"Oh, yes, without a doubt. There's opportunity for everyone down here, especially Flagler."

"How so?" asked one.

"Why, they say he's got plans for everything. He's talking about giving away citrus and vegetable seed to farmers so they can start farms up and down the coast, building more hotels, setting up water and electric companies, starting new cities. He's also involved in digging a canal that will make it possible to take a boat right up to Jacksonville without ever going onto the open ocean! Yes sir, Flagler's going to pave this place with gold, and only a fool would miss the opportunity to snatch a piece of it."

"Hear! Hear! A toast to progress! To profit!" one of the men exclaimed and raised a glass. The other men clicked their glasses together and they drank a toast.

"And you know," another continued after they had all sipped their drinks, "this isn't like out West. The Indians here aren't dangerous. And what few locals there are have no organization to speak of. No, fellows, this land is wide open for the taking and I, for one, plan on doing the taking."

I was overcome with a sudden feeling of shame. I was about to turn and walk away when Papa moved first. He whirled around and froze when he saw me standing behind him, listening. He gave me a look I shall likely never forget—full of disappointment—and then nodded at me.

"Charlie," he said. "Excuse me."

Then he walked past me, heading straight for the double doors and out of the dining room.

***

I found Papa standing on the lakeshore a little ways off the path that led to the hotel dock. His black shiny shoes were half buried in wet sand. He was looking out over the moonlit lake.

"Papa?" I said.

He turned to look at me, then back out over the water. "Charlie."

I stepped off the path to join him, the sand sucking at my own dress shoes. "Are you upset with me?"

He looked down at me, his eyebrows creased in surprise and confusion. "Upset with you? What for?"

I paused and thought about my next words. I was all mixed up with emotion, feeling ashamed and guilty when I remembered how proud I was to work for Mr. Flagler. "Do you hate Mr. Flagler, Papa?"

He laughed despite his heavy mood. "Hate him? Why, Charlie, whatever would I hate him for? He's been generous with us. He bought us these clothes. He gave you work. And I haven't seen Mama this happy in a long time. I believe she would dress up and go to a fancy ball every night if she could."

Now it was my turn to smile. "Yes. But ... if he hadn't come here, none of this would have happened."

"Is that what you think?" Papa said. "I think you've forgotten one of the first things we learned from Mr. Flagler and Mr. Ingraham. Remember, Mr. Ingraham was first hired by Henry Plant from Tampa to find a way to run a railroad across the swamp so he could come here and build hotels. Turns out Flagler just beat him to it."

126

"So it's Mr. Plant's fault?"

Papa sighed. "I'm not sure I understand what you mean by 'fault.' It's no one's fault. I believe most of our neighbors would agree with those men in there. I daresay men like Cap Dimick will be happy about all this. You heard what they said. The value of land here is bound to skyrocket. Even Hypoluxo Island will likely become very valuable."

"But we won't lose it, right?" I asked, nervous. "Not like when Gleason tried to take it?"

"No, no," Papa said. "We won't sell it unless we want to."

"Then why are you upset? If it's no one's fault

128

… and our land will become worth more … I don't really understand."

Papa didn't answer right away. "Here's the thing I want you to understand, Charlie. Mr. Flagler is not a bad man. Mr. Flagler is very likely a great man. In a hundred years, I'm certain people will remember the name Flagler. He's the kind of man who looks at a situation and sees how he can shape it to his liking. That kind of thinking is rare in a man. It's even rarer to find a man who has the willpower and the means to make it happen. It's called vision, and most people are powerfully attracted to it. Mr. Flagler has it in abundance."

I found myself nodding along. Papa was describing exactly how I'd felt about Mr. Flagler since that first day I met him, when he pointed to the wooded lakeshore and described his grand vision to me.

"But I'm a different kind of man," Papa said. "I suppose you could say I'm the kind of man who sees a wild place like this, and instead of thinking of ways I can profit from it, I think about ways I can protect and preserve it. Because I believe it's worth protecting and preserving."

Papa rested a hand on my shoulder and smiled at me, his eyes tinged with sadness. "I'm not trying to stop progress, Charlie. All Mama and I want for you and your sister is for your life to be easier and better than our own. That's what parents do. But a big part of me, maybe most of me, believes that a better life includes protecting

the gifts we've been given, including this place. That means not letting men like those you heard inside come down here and buy up, dig up, and rip up our woods without a second thought for what already lives here, both man and animal." He paused. "If I had a crystal ball, Charlie, I have a feeling that I'd see many thousands of men walking through the door Mr. Flagler has opened, and one day, maybe not too long from now, we won't recognize this land of ours."

"That sounds sad," I said.

"Yes. But there's something you can do," he said. "You can be a voice to help protect it. You and your sister. You can do that, because you will remember what we had here before all this." He swept his hand in front of us to include the lights glimmering across the lake, the hotel behind us, the boats out on the water with their lanterns swinging and the laughter of partygoers carrying toward us. "You will do that, won't you, Charlie?"

"Yes, Papa."

He pulled a foot from the sand with a sucking noise. "Now, I believe I'm ready to go home. Maybe you can go back inside and find your Mama and Lillie and we can take our leave. This will all be here tomorrow and every day after that."

Chapter Fifteen

Paradise

Lillie was at the same table where I'd left her, when Mama and I found her. She had a tray of fancy cake in front of her. She'd eaten most of it already and was happily licking icing off her fingers as Mama and I came to tell her it was time to go.

"Where'd you get that?" I asked, looking at the tray.

"I got one of the waiters to leave it," she said. "It's not like they're going to run out of food. I've been watching them come out of the kitchen. There's no end to the sweets. Besides, I told you I was hungry."

Mama smiled. "Did you enjoy the party?"

"It wasn't as bad as I thought," Lillie said, grudgingly. "This here is called Poinciana Cake. It's really delicious. And I never had to dance."

I laughed. "C'mon. Let's go."

We headed to the front doors. The

crowd was still loud and excited, and I was disappointed I hadn't seen Mr. Flagler or Mr. Ingraham. Just when I'd given up, a man rang a bell to get everyone's attention. Mr. Flagler appeared and took a position just inside the doors, next to a poster set up on a stand and covered with a sheet. Two attendants stood behind him and a crowd quickly formed. He was also dressed in a waistcoat and tailcoat and wore a broad smile beneath his top hat.

"I wanted to thank you all for coming this evening," he began. "I know most of you have traveled a great distance, and we hope you're finding the hotel to your liking—"

"Hear! Hear!" someone shouted, and the crowd all joined in cheering Mr. Flagler.

He waited until they fell quiet and then started again. "This first night kicks off what we expect will be the first of many seasons here at the Hotel Royal Poinciana. For here in South Florida, we find ourselves in one of the last unspoiled paradises in this great country of ours!"

There was more clapping and cheering.

"Now, for those of you who know me well, you know I'm not one to give grand speeches. I wouldn't want to delay dinner." There was more laughter in the crowd. "But I wanted to take a moment to thank you and to unveil the results of a little competition we've had." Here he fixed Lillie with a penetrating glance, and I guessed what was underneath the sheet. My heart began to beat faster in expectation. "We sponsored a drawing contest to see who could draw the best representation of this place. I'm proud to announce the results now!" He whipped the sheet off the poster, and everyone applauded as the poster was revealed. "The prize goes to Miss Lillie Pierce!"

And there was Lillie's alligator, right under a drawing of the hotel. The words "HOTEL ROYAL POINCIANA" were imprinted above the hotel.

Lillie must have forgotten how much cake she'd eaten, because she started jumping up and down and grabbed me. "I just won fifty dollars!" she said into my ear. "Fifty dollars, Charlie!"

"We'll leave this poster up here tonight," Mr. Flagler told the crowd, "so you can see it at your leisure. We'll be selling postcard-sized versions as well, so you can spread the word!"

This was met with more clapping, and Mr. Flagler began to work his way through the crowd as it broke up. He was shaking hands and accepting congratulations—and I soon realized he was working his way toward us. We waited until the people around him thinned and he stood looking down on me and Lillie, still smiling.

"Thank you, Mr. Flagler!" Lillie said, all of her feelings about the alligator forgotten now that she'd won.

"Thank you, Miss Lillie, for such a terrific contribution to the Hotel Royal Poinciana," he said. Then he looked at me and Mama. "And thank you for attending this evening. Charlie, a special thanks to you for all you've done. What do you think of the hotel?"

"It's ... incredible, sir," I said as Mama nodded with me.

"I'm glad to hear it!" He laughed. "Mrs. Pierce, if you don't mind, I'd like to borrow Charlie for a moment. I have a special treat for him as well. Something I suspect he'll like very much."

Mama knew Papa was waiting, but she smiled and nodded. "Yes, of course. Charlie, we'll be outside."

Mr. Flagler motioned for me to follow and led me deeper into the hotel. I wondered where we were heading as he unlocked a door with a large key and led me through. There were stairs here, and we began to climb. I'd never climbed so many stairs before and wondered if we'd come out onto the roof.

When we reached the top of the stairs, we found another locked door. Mr. Flagler opened this one into a small room that had even steeper steps going up to a trapdoor. We climbed these, and he flung the trapdoor open so we could climb out. As I emerged into the small space overhead and felt the cool night air, I realized where we were: we had climbed all the way to the top of the big tower that rose more than a hundred feet over

134

the grounds, the one I had told Mr. Flagler I wanted to climb.

I emerged onto the tower platform and my heart tightened in my chest. It was exactly as I had imagined, but so much more thrilling. My stomach felt weightless. I was higher than the tallest tree, higher than the birds flitting through the jungle and the grounds far below me. Laughter and music rose to us, sounding distant and small. The people below looked like dolls.

At the end of the great avenue, the lake glowed in moonlight, and I could see my family gathered on the shore. Out on the water, the boats with their lanterns sailed across the lake. And beyond that, on the far shore, another

cluster of lights showed where the train waited to take Mr. Flagler's guests back north.

Past the little pools of light, the dark jungle spread in every direction, and the night sky looked so close I felt as though I could raise my hand into the stars. The jungle looked wild and primitive from up here, and I imagined the animals sleeping in their burrows, unaware of the plans of us humans. The panthers and possums and alligators. The great swamp Pa-Hay-Okee off in the western distance.

"Well?" Mr. Flagler said. "Is it what you had hoped for?"

"Yes!" I said enthusiastically. "It's like … flying!"

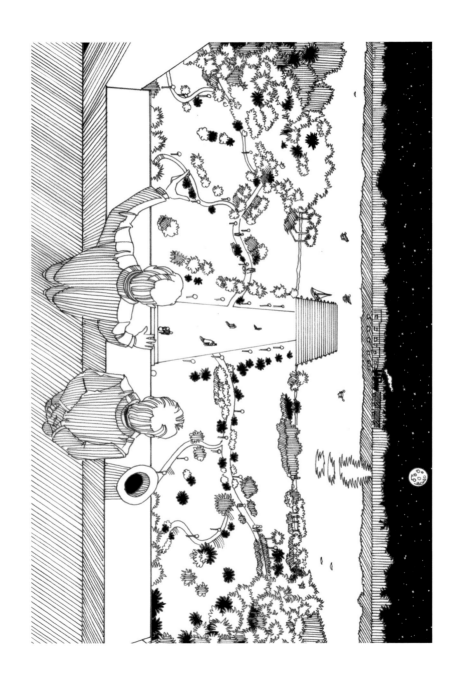

He laughed. "As I said, Charlie, I do enjoy your enthusiasm. It reminds me again why it's worth it to push against the status quo."

He looked across the lake at the little town of Westpalmbeach. "I expect one day we'll be able to stand here and see a real city across the lake."

"Yes, sir." I paused. "Our guide said you were planning to expand the hotel. Is that true?"

Flagler looked at me. "Why, yes it is, Charlie. I've got great plans for this place. We're going to add rooms. Expand the pier. Maybe build an inn on the beach with a trolley connecting the two hotels." He pointed to the train station. "You see that train? Not too long from now, we'll be able to drive that train across the lake on a new bridge we're designing. People will be able to step off their private train cars directly into the hotel lobby."

"You're going to build a bridge across the lake?" I said, some of my excitement draining away.

"Yes, that's the plan," he said. I could feel him looking at me, puzzled. "You don't sound very happy about that."

"The inlet is up north of here. How will we be able to get our boats past the bridge?"

"That's a good question, young man. You know there's a canal project heading down this way. Soon enough, all these waterways will be connected, with inlets all along the shore."

"Oh."

We fell silent for a second, taking in the sights. I tried hard to enjoy the view, but everything Papa said was bubbling up in me, and his words were still fresh in my mind. They pushed against the pride I felt at standing here on top of the world and the staggering thought that I had played a part, however small, in building something as magnificent as the hotel.

"Mr. Flagler, sir?" I said. He looked at me, and I wasn't sure how to put my thoughts into words. "What's going to happen? I mean, when the bridge is built, and the canal, and new hotels. The new town. What's going to happen to the lake? The jungle?"

"I'm not sure I understand, son," he said.

"It's just that ... my papa ... he says that everything will change. That maybe we won't recognize this place for much longer."

I was afraid Mr. Flagler would be angry, but instead he nodded in acknowledgment.

"I understand your papa's concerns," he said. "And that's very likely true. But, Charlie, change is the only constant in this life. To my thinking, every person has a choice to make. They can try to hold the change back, which is just as hopeless as trying to hold back the tide. Or they can take a part in shaping that change."

"I'm not sure I understand," I said.

"No, I would suppose not yet. You know, I've been fortunate, and my fortune has been created by hard work. But I don't think you and I are so different. I feel strongly about this place, just like you. I knew from the first time I came down here that it was a paradise. I'd like to share it with as many people as I can. I think you'll find it's very exciting, Charlie. You never know. Someday your great-great-grandchildren may still live here, and who knows what kind of world they will inherit? The best thing you can do is try to make their world a better place than you found it."

I nodded, my mind whirling with all these new thoughts. In some ways, Mr. Flagler sounded exactly like Papa, but different. I could feel the power of his vision pushing forward like a locomotive, pulling behind it the hopes and dreams of a thousand men. Everyone from Haley Mickens and his concession to A. F. Gonzalez and his friends wading across the swamp to those men in the dining room toasting profit and progress. All of them were caught up in Mr. Flagler's vision.

And I was caught up in it too. It was exciting—I was proud to be a Flagler man and wanted to help shape that future he talked about. But now I saw that Papa was right too. In all that change, someone would have to protect the land and the animals. The Florida jungle was worth fighting for. Our home was worth protecting. And just like Papa had asked, I would help protect it.

"Sir," I said, "how do we know if what we're

doing is the right thing? If it really will leave the world a better place?"

He smiled at me.

"The fact you're asking that question means you're already on the right track. All we can do is our best, Charlie. That's the most anyone can ask."

I nodded, silently promising that I would always do my best. For a second, standing on top of the world, I could imagine how the land would look in the future: the big hotels full of people, a bustling city called Westpalmbeach across the lake, railroads and ships full of people coming down here to see the beaches, the wild lands, and the great swamp. And I wondered about my own family—would they still live here? Would there be another boy someday, standing on the shore of this very lake and looking out at the water? What would he see?

I hoped it was possible that Mr. Flagler and Papa could both be right, and the word that would rise to this boy's lips in the distant future would be the same one so many people used to describe the wild jungles of South Florida:

Paradise.

Who were Flagler, Plant, Ingraham, and Gonzalez?

HENRY FLAGLER

Henry Flagler was born in Hopewell, New York, on January 2, 1830. Henry's father, Reverend Isaac Flagler, served as a pastor in the Presbyterian Church, while his mother, Elizabeth, raised Henry and his three half sisters and one half brother.

Henry grew up poor and vowed that he would make his own fortune. When he was just fourteen years old, Henry decided to strike off on his own. He traveled alone to Bellevue, Ohio, where he took a job working with his cousins and older half brother in the L. G. Harkness and Company grain store. Henry started as a clerk, working six days a week. He earned five dollars per week, plus room and board. He worked long hours and sometimes slept in the store under newspapers to save money on a blanket.

While he was at the store, he fell in love with Mary Harkness. They got married in 1853, when Henry was twenty-three years old.

141

Henry and Mary had three children: Jennie Louise, Carrie, and Henry. Sadly, Carrie died in childhood, and Jennie Louise and her newborn baby both died in 1889. Henry Flagler would later build the Memorial Presbyterian Church in St. Augustine in her honor.

While he was still young, Henry showed that he was not afraid to take risks. He started a few businesses early on, and along the way met the friend who would change his life: John D. Rockefeller.

When Flagler and Rockefeller met, the oil business was still new and there was a huge demand for refined gasoline. On January 10, 1870, Flagler and Rockefeller partnered with one of Flagler's relatives to create the company

that would become the Standard Oil Company. Standard Oil quickly became one of the largest refineries and oil companies in America. Both Rockefeller and Flagler became millionaires.

In 1878, however, misfortune fell on the Flagler family. That year, Henry Flagler's wife, Mary, became seriously ill. Her doctors recommended that she needed warm weather to get better, so the family traveled to the town of Jacksonville, Florida, for the winter.

Tragically, after spending several winters in Florida, Mary died at age forty-seven in 1881. Upset by the death of his beloved wife, Henry began to look for new business opportunities in Florida. Soon, he invested in railroads and hotels in the Tampa area on the advice of his friend and colleague Henry Plant.

In 1883, two years after Mary died, Flagler married his second wife, Ida Alice Shourds. Shortly after their wedding, he and Alice traveled to the remote settlement of St. Augustine. Flagler liked St. Augustine so much he decided to build a hotel there.

This decision marked the beginning of an incredible period of growth for Florida. Flagler opened the five-hundred-and-forty-room Hotel Ponce de Leon on January 10, 1888. Guests could reach the hotel on Flagler's brand new railroad. The Hotel Ponce de Leon cost $2.5 million to build and transformed

St. Augustine from a sleepy beach town into a resort for America's wealthy. He soon built another hotel in St. Augustine.

But Flagler wasn't done. He next built a railroad bridge across the St. Johns River and extended his railroad all the way to Ormond Beach, where he purchased the Hotel Ormond.

In 1893, Flagler purchased land on the eastern shore of Lake Worth and started construction on the Hotel Royal Poinciana. The Hotel Royal Poinciana opened in February 1894. Once again, Flagler's new hotel was a smashing success. The Hotel Royal Poinciana would eventually become the largest wooden structure in the world.

Only two years later, Flagler opened a second luxury hotel nearby on the beach, called the Palm Beach Inn. The Palm Beach Inn would later be re-named The Breakers and still stands today as one of the finest luxury hotels in the United States.

Meanwhile, a bad freeze in 1894–1895 convinced Flagler that he should keep heading south. In 1896, Flagler's railroad—now called the Florida East Coast Railway—reached Biscayne Bay. Once there, Flagler helped create a new town. The original settlers who lived there wanted to call the new town "Flagler," but Flagler suggested another name: Miami.

The town of Miami was incorporated in 1896. One year later, Flagler opened the Hotel Royal Palm, yet another luxury hotel.

By now, Flagler was a very wealthy man with a long career. Yet he still wasn't done. In 1905, Flagler announced he wanted to extend his railroad down the island chain of the Florida Keys, all the way to Key West. This extension included 156 miles of track, most of it over the open ocean. This project was considered the most ambitious construction project ever undertaken by a private citizen. Flagler called the railroad extension the Over-Sea Railroad.

After seven years of construction, the first train rolled into Key West on January 22, 1912. Thousands of people were waiting to cheer Mr. Flagler's arrival on the railway he had built.

Just over a year later, Flagler fell down a flight of stairs at his home in Palm Beach. He never recovered from his injuries, and on May 20, 1913, Henry Flagler died. He was eighty-three years old. Flagler was laid to rest in St. Augustine, next to his daughters Jennie Louise and Carrie and his first wife, Mary Harkness.

Today, Henry Flagler is credited with inventing modern Florida. Before Flagler arrived, there were few people living in Florida's wild jungles. By the time he died, Flagler had built a railroad that connected Key West to Jacksonville. He had built a string of luxury hotels, created power and water companies, encouraged all

kinds of agriculture, and helped develop the Intracoastal Waterway.

He also built a mansion in Palm Beach called Whitehall as a wedding gift for his third wife, Mary Lily Kenan. Today, Whitehall is home to the Henry Morrison Flagler Museum, a National Historic Landmark.

In 1917, the State of Florida honored Flagler with the creation of Flagler County along the Atlantic coast. Then, in 1968, the original Hotel Ponce de Leon in St. Augustine was purchased by one of Flagler's descendants, Lawrence Lewis Jr., and converted into Flagler College.

To those who worked with him, Flagler was known as a sincere and modest person. There are many stories of his helping workers who needed it. He was also a demanding employer—Flagler was known to personally visit his projects and could be deeply involved in even the smallest details.

Today, we know him as the father of modern Florida.

HENRY PLANT

Henry Plant was born October 27, 1819, in Branford, Connecticut, to a family of well-to-do farmers. Plant spent the early part of his career working for steamship companies and railroads—until the Civil War loomed. At the time, Plant was working for a railroad company called Adams Express. Adams was

headquartered in the North and they worried that the Confederate Army would take over its railroads in the South. The company agreed to sell Plant all of its southern railroads for $500,000. During the war, Plant's railroad acted as an official agent for the Confederacy, although Plant himself spent most of the war overseas in Europe.

Plant returned to the United States after the war and found the South was mostly destroyed. He began buying more bankrupt railroads and building a railroad network throughout the southern Atlantic states.

In 1882, Plant organized the Plant Investment Company. Henry Flagler was one of the investors. This company was created to build railroads and hotels throughout northern and central Florida. Between 1887 and 1898, Henry Plant built or bought hotels in Sanford, Punta Gorda, Tampa, Kissimmee, Ocala, and Fort Myers.

Plant was especially active in Tampa, which had only 750 inhabitants when he arrived in the early 1880s. Before long, Plant started a steamboat line and built the enormous Tampa Bay Hotel, which opened in 1891 at a cost of $3 million. The Tampa Bay Hotel was a magnificent resort. It had the first elevator in Florida, and its rooms were the first in the state to offer electric lights and telephone. The hotel was built in the style of a Moorish castle. Later, the hotel would be headquarters for the U.S. military during the Spanish-American War. It closed in 1930 during the Great Depression but reopened in 1933 when the Tampa Bay Junior College moved in. Today, the old hotel building houses the University of Tampa as well as the Henry B. Plant Museum.

JAMES INGRAHAM

The name James Ingraham comes up over and over in Florida history. Ingraham was born on November 18, 1850. He became a railroad engineer after graduating college.

Ingraham first traveled to Florida in 1874 as an employee of the Sanford Telegraph Company, which was owned by General Henry S. Sanford. While at Sanford, Ingraham helped build a railroad connecting Sanford, Florida, with Kissimmee. Ingraham served as president of the new railway. During that time, Henry Plant bought a majority interest in the railroad, and Ingraham helped expand the railway to Tampa, Gainesville, and High Springs.

In 1892, Florida pioneer Julia Tuttle, who lived on Biscayne Bay near present-day Miami, approached Henry Plant about bringing his railroad from the west side of the state, across the Everglades, and down to Biscayne Bay. Plant sent Ingraham on an expedition to see if this was possible. According to an essay Ingraham later wrote, this team spent almost a month paddling through the mostly unexplored swamp. After the difficult and dangerous trip, Ingraham announced it would not be possible to build a railroad through the Everglades, but he thought it would be possible to run railroad tracks down the east coast.

This didn't help Plant much—his railroad was on the other side of the state. But Henry Flagler was very interested. Flagler immediately hired Ingraham and put him in charge of land development along the east coast.

For the rest of his career, Ingraham worked closely with Flagler to push the Florida East Coast Railway further and further south. After the freeze of 1894, which wiped out crops throughout Florida, including citrus groves near Palm Beach, Flagler gave his trusted lieutenant $100,000 in cash and told him to spread it around the local farmers and laborers so no one would go hungry.

Later in his career, Ingraham served as mayor of St. Augustine from 1915 to 1920.

James Ingraham died on October 25, 1924. He is buried in St. Augustine.

ALFONSO GONZALEZ

Alfonso Fernando Gonzalez was a true Florida pioneer. He was born in 1874 in Fort Myers, Florida, when there were just a handful of people in the tiny settlement. His father was Captain Manuel Gonzalez, who had founded Fort Myers in 1866 on the site of a former Seminole Indian War fort.

When Alfonso was born, Fort Myers was a wild jungle. In 1893, when he was only nineteen years old, Alfonso joined an expedition to cross the Everglades and find work on Henry Flagler's hotel and railroad projects. The trip was supposed to take four days, but but it took fifteen. The group ended up traveling on foot through some of the roughest, wettest terrain in the United States. They faced down "thousands of moccasin snakes," ran out of food, and were forced to live on cabbage palm hearts.

The little group emerged from the swamp near Jupiter. They came upon two men cutting railroad ties for Flagler's railroad. The men were so frightened by the sight of these ragged travelers that they ran away. Gonzalez and his friends followed the men to a little store, where they got food and drink. Gonzalez later wrote that they slept almost twenty-four hours.

After they woke up, the men headed south to the Hotel Royal Poinciana, and each found work. Gonzalez went to work on one of the dredges digging the canal system that would later become the Intracoastal Waterway.

In an 1893 essay called "The Three-Mile Canal Fishes," Gonzalez wrote that his group didn't see much game as they traveled across the Everglades. Years after the trip was over, Gonzalez asked a Seminole chief about why there were so many snakes but so few game animals. The chief told Gonzalez that a big ship had sunk near where they were traveling, and that "some big snakes on board were washed onshore."

"This ended a trip I never want to make again," Gonzalez wrote.

Palm Beach Poinciana Cake

When it opened, the Hotel Royal Poinciana quickly became known as one of the finest hotels in the United States. Hotel guests were treated to the best of everything—including food and desserts.

If you want to try the same cake Lillie Pierce enjoyed at the hotel's grand opening in Chapter 15, here is the recipe for the Palm Beach Poinciana Cake. This recipe was first published in *The Southern Cookbook* in the 1920s, but the recipe itself is probably much older and was likely served in the hotel.

According to the original recipe, it was "Dainty, Delectable, Delicious."

Palm Beach Poinciana Cake

Cake

1 lb. sugar
1 lb. flour (about 3¼ cups)
1 lb. butter
The juice from 1 lemon, plus rind
9 eggs, separated
2 cups chopped, blanched almonds
½ lb. citron (can substitute with lemons)
½ lb. raisins, chopped

Cream butter and sugar and add to well-beaten egg yolks. Beat the egg whites to stiff peaks and alternate folding into the creamed butter and sugar with the flour. Dredge the fruits and nuts with flour and add to the batter. Add to two cake pans and bake at 300°F for 40–50 minutes.

Cake filling

2 cups sugar
1 cup boiling water
Juice and grated rind of two lemons
1 Tbs. corn starch
2 cups grated coconut

DIRECTIONS

Bring first three ingredients to a boil. Meanwhile, dissolve cornstarch in a little bit of cold water. Cook until it spins a thread, and beat filling until creamy. Add coconut and spread the filling between cake layers.

Thanks to John M. Blades, Executive Director Emeritus of the Henry Morrison Flagler Museum in Palm Beach, Florida, for providing this recipe. For more information about the museum, please visit: www.flaglermuseum.us

152

About Charlie Pierce

Charles William Pierce was born in Waukegan, Illinois, in 1864 and moved with his parents to Jupiter, Florida, in 1872 at the age of eight when his father was given the job as assistant keeper of the Jupiter Lighthouse. At the time, the geographical area that today comprises Palm Beach County was still part of Dade County (Palm Beach County was not created until 1909) and was inhabited only by Native Americans and escaped former slaves. The only white residents were the keeper and assistant keepers of the Jupiter Lighthouse. The Pierce family homesteaded Hypoluxo Island in 1873. In 1876, Charlie's father served as the first keeper of the Orange Grove House of Refuge, located in modern-day Delray Beach, where the Pierce family housed sailors shipwrecked along the beach. It was here that Charlie's sister, Lillie, was born in August 1876. She was the first white child born between Jupiter and Miami, an area that contains approximately seven million people today. Pierce grew up in the jungle wil-

153

derness that was South Florida prior to the arrival of Henry Flagler's Florida East Coast Railway some two decades later. The Pierces were one of the three families that salvaged the 1878 wreck of the *Providencia*, a Spanish ship carrying twenty thousand coconuts. The Pierces helped plant the coconuts that would later give Palm Beach, West Palm Beach, and Palm Beach County their names.

During his long, illustrious life as a pioneer settler of South Florida, Pierce served in many capacities, most notably as one of the legendary Barefoot Mailmen who carried the mail from

Left to right: Margretta M. Pierce; Hannibal D. Pierce; Andrew W. Garnett; James "Ed" Hamilton; Lillie E. Pierce; and Charles W. Pierce at the Pierce family home on Hypoluxo Island, ca 1886. *Photo courtesy of Historical Society of Palm Beach County*

Palm Beach to Miami and back each week. In all, the Barefoot Mailmen covered 136 miles

proximately 7,000 miles per year. They were paid six hundred dollars per year in salary. Pierce served for more than forty years as the postmaster of Boynton Beach after moving to the area in 1895, more than twenty years before the city was incorporated. His son, Charles, was the first child born in Boynton Beach. Pierce served on the boards of various community organizations, as president of the first bank organized in Boynton

The mailman in this mural titled *The Barefoot Mailman*, by Stevan Dohanos, is said to resemble Charlie Pierce. *Photo courtesy of Historical Society of Palm Beach County*

round trip in six days, rested on Sunday, and then started anew on Monday, for a total of ap-

Beach, and as master of the first Masonic Lodge. His childhood adventures were accurately recorded, and his writings remain today one of the best firsthand accounts of early exploration in southeast Florida. Pierce was farsighted enough to maintain a daily journal from early childhood until late in his life. These journal entries provide the foundation for his book, *Pioneer Life in Southeast Florida*, which is the most comprehensive account of the pioneer settlement of South Florida and is the primary reference for most subsequent books on the region's history. Pierce died in 1939 at age seventy-four while still serving as the postmaster of Boynton Beach. Pierce Hammock Elementary School in Palm Beach County is named in his honor. In 2009, the State of Florida posthumously named Charles

Charles Pierce at his desk, ca 1930. *Photo courtesy of Historical Society of Palm Beach County*

Pierce a "Great Floridian," one of fewer than seventy people in Florida's history granted the title. Florida Governor Charlie Crist performed the induction.

About the Author

Harvey E. Oyer III

Harvey E. Oyer III is a fifth-generation Floridian and is descended from one of the earliest pioneer families in South Florida. He is the great-great-grandson of Captain Hannibal Dillingham Pierce and his wife, Margretta Moore Pierce, who in 1872 became one of the first non-Native American families to settle in southeast Florida. Oyer is the great-grandnephew of Charlie Pierce, the subject of this book. Oyer is an attorney in West Palm Beach, Florida, a Cambridge University-educated archaeologist, and an avid historian. He served for many years as the chairman of the Historical Society of Palm Beach County, currently serves on the board of the Florida Historical Society, has written or contributed to numerous books and articles about Florida history, and was named a Florida Distinguished Author in 2013. Many of the stories contained in this book have been passed down through five generations of his family.

For more information about the author, Harvey E. Oyer III, or Charlie Pierce and his adventures, go to **www.TheAdventuresofCharliePierce.com**.

Become a friend of Charlie Pierce on **Facebook**.

Visit The Adventures of Charlie Pierce website at
www.TheAdventuresofCharliePierce.com

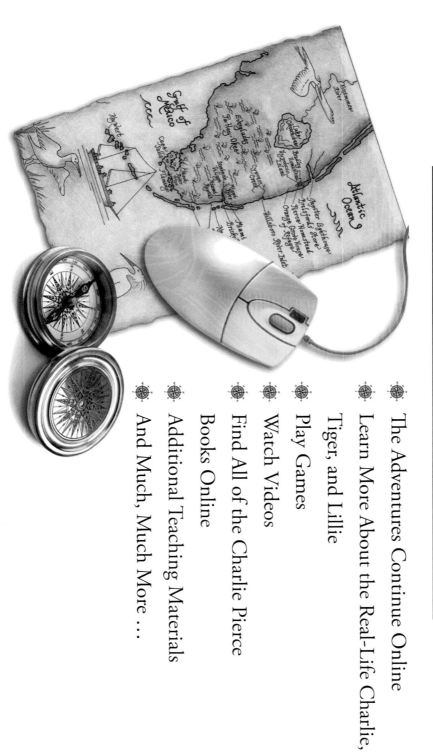

- The Adventures Continue Online
- Learn More About the Real-Life Charlie, Tiger, and Lillie
- Play Games
- Watch Videos
- Find All of the Charlie Pierce Books Online
- Additional Teaching Materials
- And Much, Much More …

The Adventures of Charlie Pierce Collection

The Adventures of Charlie Pierce: The American Jungle

In 1872, eight-year-old Charlie Pierce arrived with his Mama and Papa in the frontier jungles of South Florida. In this account, based on actual diaries, Charlie explores old battlefields, faces down hurricanes, and makes an incredible discovery in the sand.

The Adventures of Charlie Pierce: The Last Egret

In the late nineteenth century, hunters killed millions of birds in the Florida Everglades to supply the booming trade in bird feathers for ladies' fashion. As teenagers, Charlie Pierce and his friends traveled deep into the unexplored Florida Everglades to hunt plume birds for their feathers. They never imagined what they would learn about themselves and how they would contribute to American history.

The Adventures of Charlie Pierce: The Last Calusa

When famous scientist Dr. George Livingston shows up in the steamy jungles of Florida, he offers to pay Charlie Pierce to take him deep into the Everglades in search of the rare ghost orchid. But it doesn't take long before the expedition discovers that the swamp is hiding much more than a rare flower as the oldest legends suddenly spring to life.

The Adventures of Charlie Pierce: The Barefoot Mailman

Charlie Pierce isn't looking for an adventure when he agrees to help out his friend and neighbor Ed Hamilton. Hamilton's job is to walk the U.S. Mail from Palm Beach to Miami and back every week. When Hamilton goes missing, it's up to Charlie and his sister, Lillie, to find out what happened to the missing Barefoot Mailman.

The Adventures of Charlie Pierce: Charlie and the Tycoon

When industrialist Henry Flagler arrives in Florida in the late 19th century, the state is a wild jungle with few people. But that changes quickly as Flagler builds hotels and railroads down the Atlantic coast — with the help of teenaged Charlie Pierce. Along the way, Charlie and his family realize that building the future means saying goodbye to the Florida they know and love.

Awards for The Adventures of Charlie Pierce

Florida Publishers Association

Gold Medal - Children's Fiction (*The American Jungle*, 2010)
Gold Medal - Florida Children's Book (*The American Jungle*, 2010)
Gold Medal - Children's Fiction (*The Last Egret*, 2011)
Silver Medal - Florida Children's Book (*The Last Egret*, 2011)
Gold Medal - Florida Children's Book (*The Last Calusa*, 2013)
Silver Medal - Children's Fiction (*The Last Calusa*, 2013)
Gold Medal - Fiction/Non-Fiction: Juvenile (*The Barefoot Mailman*, 2015)

James J. Horgan Award (Florida Historical Society)

(*The Last Egret*, 2011)
(*The Last Calusa*, 2013)

Florida Book Award

Bronze Medal - Children's Literature (*The Last Egret*, 2010)

Mom's Choice Awards

Silver Medal (*The Last Egret*, 2010)